DELPHINE
AND THE
DARK THREAD

Praise for

DELPHINE
AND THE
SILVER NEEDLE

by Alyssa Moon

"Filled with action, adventure, humor, and magic, *Delphine and the Silver Needle* stitches together a fantastical tale that will keep you turning the pages well after midnight."
—MARI MANCUSI, author of the *Camelot Code* and *Dragon Ops* series

"There's more to the mice in Cinderella's château than anyone knew, with Delphine lighting the way to a brand-new epic fantasy series!"
—JAMES RILEY, *New York Times* best-selling author of the *Half Upon a Time, Story Thieves,* and *Revenge of Magic* series

"A delight of a quest story that will fill the need of readers seeking a fractured fairy tale, talking animals, or just a quick-moving adventure."
—*School Library Journal*

"Disney's *Lord of the Rings* for tweens."   —*Laughing Place*

DELPHINE
AND THE
DARK THREAD

ALYSSA MOON

Disney • HYPERION
LOS ANGELES   NEW YORK

First Edition, March 2022
10 9 8 7 6 5 4 3 2 1
FAC-021131-22014
Printed in the United States of America

This book is set in Baskerville MT Pro/Monotype; Caslon Antique/Monotype; Copperplate
Gothic LT Pro/Monotype; Elaina Script/Fontspring; Isabel Unicase/Fontspring
Designed by Marci Senders
Illustrations by Therese Larsson © Disney Enterprises, Inc.

Library of Congress Cataloging-in-Publication Data

Names: Moon, Alyssa, author.
Title: Delphine and the dark thread / by Alyssa Moon.
Description: First edition. • Los Angeles ; New York : Disney-Hyperion,
2022. • Series: Delphine • Audience: Ages 8–12. • Audience: Grades 4–6.
• Summary: Delphine the seamstress mouse uses her needle's ancient magic
to save the kingdom from King Midnight.
Identifiers: LCCN 2021007971 (print) • LCCN 2021007972 (ebook) •
ISBN 9781368048330 (hardcover) • ISBN 9781368063357 (ebk)
Subjects: CYAC: Magic—Fiction. • Good and evil—Fiction. • Mice—Fiction.
• Rats—Fiction. • Adventure and adventurers—Fiction.
Classification: LCC PZ7.1.M6485 Dc 2022 (print) • LCC PZ7.1.M6485 (ebook)
• DDC [Fic]—dc23
LC record available at https://lccn.loc.gov/2021007971
LC ebook record available at https://lccn.loc.gov/2021007972

Reinforced binding
Visit www.DisneyBooks.com

For Picklepop, the real Cornichonne

Prologue

The wall that had stood around the mouse city for centuries was crumbling. The invading rats were strong enough to claw straight through the stone. Inside, they streamed past the little farms toward the center of the mouse city. They ransacked homes, dragging innocent residents into the streets. Somewhere, a pinkie mouse was crying.

The rats reached the elegant city square. Broad flagstones stretched toward a stone fountain. From high above, mice watched in terror. The attackers spread, seizing torches from wall sconces. They smashed windows and threw the torches inside. Within moments, acrid smoke was curling angrily from the buildings.

At the edge of the square, a dappled mouse snuck out of a doorway, hood pulled down low. She held a scroll in one paw with a hastily scrawled warning to the other mouse cities. If she could escape unnoticed . . .

She tiptoed through the shadows, holding her breath, but a loose flagstone rattled beneath her paw. The sound was loud enough to attract the attention of the closest rat. He reached her with a single bound. She lashed out with her claws and he lashed back, throwing the mouse halfway across the square. She hit the side of the stone fountain and fell to the cobblestones.

"Find that needle!" screamed the rat leader, his fangs dripping with foam. "Find the mouse with the needle! For Midnight!"

The rats redoubled their attacks, tearing doors off hinges and ripping through walls. Screams echoed through the broad streets. No corner of the city was safe.

The mice could no longer defend their home. They turned tail and fled as the rats pursued them.

Next to the fountain at the center of the square, the dappled mouse lay crumpled against the rose vines that grew around the base. Two stone mice stood at the center of the fountain, gazing up at the golden spindle balanced between their paws.

A thin stream of shining water flowed down from the spindle like a silver thread. The dappled mouse's eyes fluttered open. With great determination, she lifted her head to look up at the stone mice. "Arachne and Rhapso, watch over my city . . . " she began, but her words came thick. She gasped and fell back to the ground.

The air around the two stone mice shimmered silver for a moment, then the silvery shimmer drifted onto the rose vines. The statues remained cold and solid. But the thorns of the rose vines were now silver.

The rats had torn apart the city and found nothing. They moved on, hunting for the mouse with the needle. They would not fail, no matter how many cities they had to destroy.

In the mouse city, the fires burned, staining the stone walls black with soot. Not until snow began to flutter downward did the flames succumb. Soon the ruins of the silent city lay under a blanket of white. Only the figures of Arachne and Rhapso remained, their stone eyes gazing into the distance.

The war had begun.

the Roquefort m●●n

Chapter 1

"Cornichonne, your face!" Delphine couldn't help laughing at the sight of the cat standing in the snow. Frozen droplets hung from her friend's short whiskers like tiny icicles.

"Yesh. This always happens to me when it's cold," Cornichonne said in her gravelly voice. She exhaled and her moist breath escaped into the wintry air, where it formed another layer of frosty crystals on her flat face.

They were standing at the mouth of an abandoned badger

burrow, looking out at the forest. The sun was so weak that it barely managed to break through the tree branches. Delphine clutched her needle, running her paws along the engravings on the shining silver shaft. Somewhere out there lay the next step on the trail of her ancestor, and perhaps the key to Delphine's true identity. But something else awaited her, too: King Midnight, the murderous rat who would stop at nothing to get his claws on Delphine's magic needle.

"Alexander?" Delphine turned and glanced back into the burrow. "Are you ready?"

"Hmm?" Alexander emerged, swirling his creamy velvet cloak around him. It was already the worse for wear after a week of living inside the dusty hole in the ground. But he held his head high and managed a courtly grin. "My lady, I am as ready as the day I slew the hawkworms."

Delphine smiled, despite her worries. The rats were still out there, searching the forests. Her mind jumped back to the terrible night they had fled Château Trois Arbres—how the rats had rampaged through the halls, taking down the mice who were there for the Winterberry Ball. Delphine had realized that the only way to protect everyone was to flee the château. She was the one the rats were after. But what had happened to Princess Petits-Oiseaux . . . and her pawmaids . . . and the footmice . . . and the princess's pet bumblebee? Delphine could only hope that they had all made it to safety.

Now Delphine feared it wouldn't be long before the rats

tracked them down in the dim wood. "Then let's get going. We've lost some time."

Cornichonne's golden eyes widened. "How long was I asleep?"

Delphine tried to remember. "Four days, I think? It's fine. You needed to rest." The cat had collapsed to the ground after they had escaped the rats, and no wonder: she had run straight through the night in order to save them.

"I do feel better," Cornichonne said with a yawn. Drool dripped from one fang onto the snow and froze.

Delphine reached up and patted her friend's tiny nose. "Good."

Delphine and Alexander strapped their makeshift saddlebags to the cat, and Delphine gave yet another silent thank-you that the ballgown she'd been wearing when they escaped included so many petticoats. She had gladly sacrificed several of them to sew into saddlebags so they could carry the roots they had dug out of the walls of the burrow. They were withered but would serve as meager rations on the road.

Delphine shivered, her paws already half-frozen through her thin silk dancing slippers. She could see Alexander was trembling as well. "We need to find better clothing," she said. Her stomach growled. "And more food. Not to mention shelter."

"Just the basics in Mouselow's Hierarchy of Needs," Alexander replied, ever cheerful.

Delphine felt grateful for his positive outlook, especially

when things were so dire. But she still couldn't stop worrying. Why *had* she been entrusted with a needle of the Threaded? For years, it had hung above her bed at Château Desjardins, on the doorstep of which she'd been found as a baby. Her maman (oh, how she missed Maman!) had kept it—as well as the cloth bundle in which she'd been wrapped—so Delphine would have mementos of her mysterious past. But until very recently, the needle had lain dormant.

Why could she now tap into the needle's ancient magic? Was it her fault that the treaty with the rats had been broken, putting the entire kingdom of Peltinore in danger from King Midnight? And if so, what could she, a mere seamstress mouse, possibly do to stop him? Maman would say that to solve any problem, one must start by finding the knot. The trouble was, everything felt so tangled. What Delphine wouldn't do to be back at Château Desjardins, talking it all through with Maman over their Friday croissant crumbs and hot barley tea.

Sighing, Delphine settled herself on Cornichonne's back and watched Alexander finish strapping his decorative scabbard around his waist. It was an elaborate affair, complete with the dress sword that had come with his ensemble for the Winterberry Ball. Luckily he also had the sharpened rat dagger he had snatched up as they fled, a dagger large enough to serve as a sword for a mouse. He tucked that one into the strap of his scabbard over the other hip and bowed in her direction.

Delphine had to laugh. "Always perfectly dressed for the occasion!" she teased as he climbed up behind her.

Cornichonne twitched one of her ears. "Which way?"

"Let's head north," Delphine replied after a moment. Cornichonne nodded and set off through the thick, dark forest.

"Why north?" said Alexander, pressed up close behind her to keep them both warm.

"It's the opposite direction from home. It's the best I could think of for now."

"Fair enough."

The ancient trees hung heavy with frozen webs of moss. Delphine began to relax as Cornichonne padded along. The cat sang softly to herself.

Pollywogs have froggy tails,
Slimier than curtain snails,
Over under over under,
Stop before you make a blunder,
Tie a tiny bow on top and go.

See a fish and make a wish,
Put it in a cooking dish,
Over under over under,
Listen for the coming thunder,
Tie a tiny bow on top and go.

The song went on like this for some time, until Delphine had stopped wondering what it all meant and started wondering how in the world Cornichonne could remember so many verses. Just then, Alexander poked his nose into the top edge of her travel cloak. It felt like someone had pressed an icicle against her neck.

"Alexander! Stop that!"

He pulled back sheepishly. "My nose is cold."

"You need a nose like mine," said Cornichonne. "Flat. It's perfect."

"Cornichonne has a nose?" Alexander stage-whispered.

"I heard that," said the cat with a snuffle.

At that moment, a growl sounded in the trees nearby. All three travelers stiffened.

"Wait—" Alexander's nose twitched. The smells of roasting potatoes and woodsmoke wafted toward them, along with more snorting sounds. They relaxed. The noises weren't growls; they were *snores*. Someone was napping by a campfire.

Alexander slid down from Cornichonne's back and drew his rat-dagger sword. "Sounds like the owner of those potatoes isn't guarding them very well," he said in a low voice. "Anyone else fancy some lunch?"

"Are you sure that's a good idea?" whispered Delphine.

"Only one way to find out." He flashed her an insouciant grin and disappeared among the trees.

Delphine hopped off Cornichonne. The cat immediately sat

down and began to groom her paws. "Aren't *you* worried?" said Delphine.

"Whatever that creature is, it's asleep," pointed out Cornichonne. She licked another chunk of ice from between her toes. "Just don't wake it up."

Delphine pushed her way between the branches in the direction Alexander had gone, following the smell of roasted vegetables. She found him peeking between the fronds of a dead fern, blocking her view.

"What do you see?" she hissed, trying to look around him.

His ears went pale. "Uh, Delfie," he whispered through clenched teeth, "I think we should go back now. No potato is worth that risk."

"Why?" She stood on tiptoe, finally managing to peer over his shoulder. A squeak of horror escaped her.

In a little clearing lay a rat next to a campfire. It was indeed asleep, its head thrown back with its mouth hanging open. As they watched, another bone-rattling snore escaped. The sight made Delphine's blood run as cold as Lucifer the cat always had back at Château Desjardins. She squeaked again.

Alexander's paw pressed against her mouth. "Shhh!"

They retreated, one slow step at a time. They had almost reached Cornichonne when an unpleasant grumble erupted behind them. The rat was waking up.

"Go!" They abandoned stealth and scrambled back onto the

cat's back. Cornichonne leapt forward and the rat sounds faded into the distance.

When they had gone far enough that the cat judged it safe to slow to a walk, Alexander began chortling.

Delphine turned on him. "What are you laughing at?"

"Who knew rats liked potatoes?"

"It's not funny, Alexander," she said, crossing her arms, but even Cornichonne was snuffling in amusement. "All right, it was a little bit funny," she said, penitent. Then she remembered something. "Did you see what it was wearing?"

"Wearing?" Alexander sounded confused. "Tan breeches, I think? And a straw hat?"

"Exactly! Not the uniform of Midnight's rats. I don't think it was one of his troops."

"A random rat, traveling through the forest in the dead of winter, like us?" She felt Alexander shrug behind her. "I suppose stranger things have happened."

They rode for a while in silence, until Delphine started smiling again. "The look on your face *was* pretty funny."

Alexander chuckled, a cheerful sound in the gloomy murk. "It'll be a good story."

✳   ✳   ✳

The forest was not only dark and murky, it was also far more overgrown and foreboding than anywhere they had yet been.

The gnarled branches of the old trees hung low like fingertips, reaching for them as they passed.

Alexander leaned forward. "So what's your plan, Delfie?"

"I'm working on it." She didn't want to admit that she had no plan at all. Find King Midnight, somehow. Figure out how to stop him. All while not getting captured by his minions swarming the countryside. And if the sheer number of rats camped around Château Trois Arbres had been any indication, he had an enormous army.

He gave her a squeeze. "You'll know what to do when the time is right."

She wished she felt as confident as he did. She was about to say so, when a sharp crack echoed through the trees.

Cornichonne froze. Delphine strained to see through the gloom.

Another *crack*, closer, as if someone had stepped on a brittle twig. Cornichonne's head silently pivoted toward a clump of undergrowth nearby.

Now they could hear heavy steps approaching, and bizarrely, a thrumming buzz. Delphine spotted something large and round floating through the gray fog toward them.

"What *is* that?" she blurted.

"Shhhhh!" Alexander hissed.

A narrow figure pushed through the branches behind the floating shape. Despite the fog, Delphine could make out a slim snout beneath a hood pulled down low.

The object was still floating straight toward them. The buzzing burned her ears, and she shook her head to try to clear it. Wind began to blow around the shape, wafting the fog away in sinuous strands of gray. She could see a blur like the beating of a beetle's wings.

They *were* wings, Delphine realized. Moving so quickly they were causing the air to shimmer. The last webs of fog melted away, and they saw a bumblebee hovering in midair, its faceted eyes like blocks of onyx staring at them. The aristocratic figure reached up to pull back her hood. Delphine gasped.

It was Ysabeau, Princess Petits-Oiseaux's pawmaid. With the princess's pet bee.

Chapter 2

Ysabeau appeared bedraggled from travel, her eyes pink with lack of sleep. But at the sight of Delphine she broke into a relieved smile. Delphine leapt from Cornichonne's back and ran across the clearing toward the pawmaid. The sight of someone from the château alive and safe made her heart grow light.

Then a terrible thought struck her. If Ysabeau was here, alone . . .

Delphine's paws flew to her mouth. "The princess . . . !"

Ysabeau shook her head. "No! Princess Petits-Oiseaux is safe."

"And the others?"

Now Ysabeau's face fell. "Not all so lucky. By the time the rats took off to track you down, they had already left a trail of carnage . . ." She shuddered. "It will take a long time before anyone feels safe at Château Trois Arbres."

The bumblebee floated nearby, his huge unblinking eyes pinned on Delphine. Ysabeau pulled a little dried flower from her pocket and he buzzed toward her.

"He likes honeysuckle," Ysabeau confided. "So I always keep a few dried blooms with me."

Delphine watched him snuffle the flower. "So that *is* Bearnois?" She looked back at Ysabeau. "What's going on?"

Ysabeau smiled wearily. "I'm glad I found you. But the rats could be anywhere. We need to keep moving." She pulled her hood back up and turned back into the forest. "Come."

The mice hurried after her, Cornichonne padding alongside. "Who is that?" the cat whispered to Alexander.

"She's one of the princess's pawmaids," Alexander responded in a low voice. "And that's the princess's bee, Bearnois. But I have no idea what they're doing in the middle of the forest. Or how they got here."

"*We* got here," pointed out Cornichonne.

"But Ysabeau didn't have a cat to ride on. Well, I suppose we *were* in that burrow for a while. But was she looking for us?"

Ysabeau turned to Alexander. "Yes. And I found you, as you can see."

Alexander's ears turned pink—clearly he'd realized that his whispers had not been inconspicuous.

Delphine winced. "Was our trail that obvious?"

"Not obvious at all," Ysabeau said. "The cat must have done a good job of covering her tracks." She glanced back again. "Is she the one you told the princess about? Cornichonne?"

Delphine nodded. She had forgotten how strange it must seem that two mice were traveling with a cat. "She's very kind," Delphine said, hoping to reassure the pawmaid.

"As well as a wonderful travel companion, it seems." Ysabeau led them through the overgrown forest with ease. It was as if she were following a path that only she could see. The difference between how she carried herself in the wilderness and how Alexander did those first few days of Delphine's quest . . . it was hard to believe they had both come from the same castle.

"And no," the pawmaid continued. "You didn't leave any tracks. Bearnois found you." At the sound of his name, the bee buzzed happily. "Bearnois can sense things. There have always been a few special bees with that ability. That's why he spends his days with the princess, to help keep her safe."

Delphine was surprised. "I thought he was her pet."

"Oh, he is!" Ysabeau laughed. "But he's also much more.

And I'm his handler." She patted Bearnois's fuzzy side. "The princess can tell whether to trust those who visit her from the pitch of his buzzing. And if she were ever attacked, he could subdue the attacker with a single sting. But it would cost him his life to do so. That's the price the royal bumblebees pay to be able to sense so deeply." Her voice had gone somber.

Delphine looked at Bearnois's dark, intelligent eyes. "What can he sense?"

"Danger. Evil. But he senses good even more strongly. Those with love and hope within. Those who would aid the princess and the kingdom. I remember when you and I first met; Bearnois had been calmer around you than with any other visitor the princess had ever had. It meant he sensed goodness inside you. Deep goodness."

"And you said he tracked me?" A plan was forming in Delphine's mind.

"He doesn't track, precisely. It's more like he *felt* where you had gone, and followed those bits of feelings."

"Aha!" Delphine moved to grab Alexander's sleeve. "Why didn't you tell me that the princess's bee could do that?"

Alexander looked confused. "I didn't tell you about the footman's great talent on the harpsichord, either. I didn't think it was relevant. The princess of the kingdom has always had a bee. It's tradition. Why does it matter?"

"Because he can lead me to Midnight!" She turned to

Ysabeau. "That's the rats' leader. He wants my needle, and his troops are going to lay waste to the kingdom until he gets it. But if I could find him first, maybe I could stop him before more innocents die."

Ysabeau was already shaking her head. "No."

"No? Why not?"

"It doesn't work that way. Bearnois can't track someone he's never met. But he also wouldn't be willing to track someone who leaves evil in their path. Evil weakens his power until it becomes useless." Ysabeau must have seen the frustration on Delphine's face. "At least he was able to bring me to you," she finished diplomatically.

"Then why *did* you want to find me?" asked Delphine.

"That's a longer story, and the sun has already gone down. Let's set up camp for the night, and I'll tell you over dinner."

✳ ✳ ✳

Ysabeau found a cozy cave in the side of a hill. She built a neat little campfire, then dug up a few acorns nearby and rolled them into the fire to cook.

Delphine watched, eyes wide. "How did you know those acorns were there?"

Ysabeau smiled. "When squirrels bury their acorns, they always mark the spot with a little round stone." She pointed at a nearby pebble. To Delphine it looked exactly like every other pebble. But somehow Ysabeau could see the difference.

Before long the acorn shells popped from the heat. They picked out the nutmeat and ate with gusto. It was the first hot food Delphine and Alexander had had since fleeing the château. They had been afraid a fire might be spotted, no matter how small. Delphine was about to ask Ysabeau if she wasn't afraid of the same thing, when she realized the firelight was contained by the ice-covered banks around them. Ysabeau had found a spot that was entirely hidden.

Ysabeau was no newcomer to the forest—Delphine was sure now. "How did you learn all these skills?"

"Ah," said Ysabeau, finishing up her acorn. "That's part of the long story I mentioned. I suppose I should start at the beginning."

Ysabeau had grown up in the country, she told them, on a farm in the northern forests of the kingdom. Not too far from where they sat now, in fact. She had spent her childhood playing in the forest, exploring deeper and deeper as she grew older. One day she stumbled across a massive stone wall. On the other side lay an entire city. It was abandoned, ruined, swallowed back up by the forest.

Alexander gasped. "One of the Dead Cities!"

Delphine shivered. She remembered listening to ghost stories about the Dead Cities as a young mouse. Jaq's grandfather would spin tale after tale late at night, as she, Jaq, and Gus curled up on the sofa. Every story described a different mouse city that had been destroyed by the rats a century ago, during the War to End All Wars.

Cornichonne's ears perked up. "Why are the cities dead?"

"They're not actually dead, just abandoned," explained Delphine. "Nobody returned after the war was over. They're out there somewhere, buried in a hundred years of forest growth."

Ysabeau nodded. "And here was a Dead City, right in front of me. I had to see what lay inside."

The mouse told them that she'd spent that day exploring the ruins. Fascinated by what she had found, she visited again the next day, and the next, until it became her secret place. She would spend hours wandering through the streets. Once, inside a grand building, she discovered a wall decorated with strange symbols carved in the stone. She studied them many times but had never been able to figure out what they meant.

"Then you arrived at Château Trois Arbres with that silver needle," finished Ysabeau. "And I recognized the markings."

Delphine pulled out her needle and stared at it. The runes? The ones she had never been able to decipher?

"Those symbols . . . they're the same ones I saw on the wall of the Dead City. It can't be a coincidence. So that's where we're going to compare your needle to those symbols. Maybe there's a clue there somehow. It wasn't my place to say anything that day in Princess Petits Oiseaux's chambers, but now there's nothing to lose."

Delphine suddenly realized what Ysabeau had done. "You left her employ."

"If I had information that could help save the kingdom, and I didn't act . . . I could never forgive myself. My family is out there, too, protected by the treaty. Or they had been, until it was broken by the rats that night at Château Trois Arbres. I told Princess Petits-Oiseaux that I had to try to find you. She said there would always be a place for me as one of her pawmaids, if I chose to return."

Alexander interrupted. "What about Bearnois?"

Ysabeau ran her paw over the bee's soft fur. "She insisted I take him. She knew I'd never be able to find you without his help."

"Still—" began Alexander, but Cornichonne cut him off.

"It was Bearnois's choice," the cat murmured. She and the bee were staring deep into each other's eyes, both unblinking. "He wanted to go. Wanted to find Delphine."

"Bees rarely bond with other animals," whispered Ysabeau, watching. "There must be something very special about your cat friend, indeed." She turned back to Delphine, all business again. "We should be at the Dead City in two days if we travel quickly. But the rats can't be far behind. We have to get there before they get to us."

Delphine's thoughts went again to Midnight. Instinctively, she reached for the needle, tracing her paw along the engraving. She realized she hadn't practiced summoning its power in some time, and it was suddenly clear what she must do: master the magic of the needle so that she could stop Midnight.

It was their only chance.

* * *

As the others picked at the remaining crumbs of acorn nutmeat, Delphine decided to spend the rest of the evening working with the needle. Excusing herself, she found a spot on the edge of the campsite and focused on summoning one sharp blast of magic at a time, aiming at a tree far away from her friends.

It wasn't as difficult as she had thought once she let her worries fall away so she could concentrate. What *was* difficult was ignoring the constant cries of "Huzzah!" from Alexander at the campsite after every single lightning bolt.

After his thirtieth *huzzah!*, she glanced over her shoulder. He beamed back, waving, blithely unaware of her growing irritation. She tried to focus again, but her mind was now split between controlling the magic and ignoring the loud cheers behind her. On her next attempt, the needle spat out a bunch of half-formed magic splurts that flopped onto the ground.

"Oh, I say!" cried Alexander. She turned around to see that he was standing on top of a stump, clapping, presumably his idea of a standing ovation. Ysabeau watched him from her seat by the fire, an amused smile on her lips.

"Alexander?" Delphine tried to keep her voice calm.

"Yes, Delfie?" he called, hopping down. "Or should I say, *Mistress of the Needle*?"

"Alexander, I *love* your enthusiasm, but . . ." She paused as she noticed the admiration on his face. Taking a deep breath, she let her irritation melt away. "Alexander, what I wanted to say is . . . I couldn't do this without you."

His ears turned dark pink, noticeable even from where she stood. "It is my honor," he replied. He swept into one of his deep bows. Unfortunately, as he reached the lowest point of his bow, the tips of his whiskers strayed into the flames of the fire.

"Nutmegs!" He leapt up, his whiskers smoking. Ysabeau grabbed her travel cloak and threw it over Alexander's head to smother the embers.

Delphine tried to suppress the urge to giggle at the sight of him standing stock-still, almost entirely hidden beneath the dark fabric. "Thank you," she heard him say in a small, muffled voice. Then, a moment later: "Ooh! Ysabeau, your cloak smells like honey!"

LYMON YAWNED AND SCRATCHED AT his chest with his long rat claws. Still half-asleep, he rolled off the straw pallet and reached for his sword belt. Another day of patrolling the streets of the city, making sure the mice didn't take more liberties with the rats than what was allowed.

That idiotic treaty. He'd lived his whole life beneath its oppression, as had his father and his father's father before him. But that was what it meant to be a rat in the kingdom of Peltinore.

He emerged onto the street to discover that not a single one of his rat crew had reported for duty yet that morning. He picked at his teeth, frowning, and decided he'd have to have a word with them. Just as he was about to go back inside and scrounge for breakfast, a commotion at the end of the street caught his attention—chickens were squawking and a flash of auburn darted straight toward him.

A fox. This was not good at all.

As it neared, it slowed, and the rat messenger riding on its back tumbled off. The fox wrinkled its nose in disgust and disappeared around a corner.

Lymon gazed down at the messenger with some degree of terror. He knew the price foxes demanded to carry rats. Two rats would have been presented, and the fox would have chosen which to carry and which to eat in payment for its service. Gruesome, but effective in keeping requests to a minimum. So whatever this message was, it had to be important.

He reached down and helped the rat stand up. Dried blood caked the sleeves of the messenger's coat. He tottered, trying to get his bearings.

"Message from Commandant Robeaux," he gasped. "The treaty is broken. All that matters is finding the mouse with the silver needle, at any cost. She could be anywhere. Leave no stone unturned."

Lymon gawped at the messenger. "The treaty is broken?"

The rat pointed at his stained sleeves. "Turns out mice bleed red like us. But the one with the needle slipped from between our claws." He wiped his forehead. "More messengers are heading out across the kingdom as we speak."

Lymon's thoughts were elsewhere, among the many tiny houses and barns of the mouse towns that studded the land outside the city walls. So many places to hide. Not to mention all the nooks and crannies inside the city proper. It would be a lot of work searching them all. But if the treaty was truly broken, well . . .

Lymon looked over at a farmer mouse who was rolling a wheel of cheese down the street with his children's help. He put a paw on his sword belt, not bothering to hide his grin. His job had just gotten a lot more fun.

CHapter 3

They walked for two days, threading their way between low-hanging icicles and branches weighted down by the snow. Ysabeau led the group once more, her hood tucked around her long, straight whiskers. Delphine followed, distracted. She was now able to summon lightning bolts with some regularity, but she knew she'd only scratched the surface when it came to the needle's magic.

Alexander's voice broke into her thoughts. "Delfie? Did you hear me?"

"Hmm?" Delphine looked over to realize he was offering her a morsel of leftover acorn nutmeat. She gratefully accepted, pulling her cloak closer against the cold.

Night would be coming soon. Delphine suddenly wondered why they weren't stopping to set up camp. Shouldn't they be scouting for a good location?

But then Ysabeau whistled and pointed through the ancient trees.

Delphine and Alexander squinted ahead as Ysabeau forged on, and after a few more paces, a shape emerged from the gloom.

A high stone wall stood in the middle of the forest.

The pale stones gleamed in the early twilight. "Built to protect the city," breathed Ysabeau as they walked closer. Alexander tipped back his head in awe, studying the parapets. "But . . ." Ysabeau pointed again, with sadness in her eyes. "Not strong enough when it was truly needed, it seems."

Delphine saw what she meant. To the west, the wall had been torn down nearly to its base; stones lay scattered around the open gash.

"That's where we'll enter."

They had nearly reached the gap when Cornichonne froze, her eyes huge. The tip of her tail jolted.

Delphine felt a twist of fear. Were the rats already here? The cat drew lower to the ground, her tail now lashing from side to side. She lunged, launching herself toward a nondescript spot on the ground. She snapped up something black in her mouth with a wet crunch. Alexander let out a little squeak.

But Ysabeau began to laugh. In another moment Cornichonne turned back around, and Delphine saw why. The long, spiny legs of a massive earwig were hanging from her mouth. She slurped up the legs, her whiskers twitching in delight.

Alexander groaned. Delphine turned to see that his ears had gone green. "Alexander! Don't tell me you still have such a delicate constitution, after being this long on the road with Cornichonne!"

"But I've never actually seen her eat something that big, or"—he swallowed hard—"with that many *legs*."

Cornichonne returned, still licking her lips. "Shall we keep going?" she asked with a toothy grin. Then she noticed Alexander's expression. "Is he all right? He didn't eat something bad, did he?"

Alexander turned away with another groan, and Delphine fought to keep her face straight. "He's fine," she promised.

When they reached the massive opening torn in the wall, Delphine could see claw marks gouging the stones. She suppressed a shudder. They looked like the marks she had seen on the walls of Château Trois Arbres the night the rats had invaded. Ysabeau helped Delphine and Alexander climb up the uneven blocks.

"Who lived here?" Delphine panted as she pulled herself up,

catching her first glimpse of the massive city inside the walls. Cottages, then larger houses and buildings, stretched away toward a town square in the distance. This close to the guard wall, the houses were small and spread far apart, surrounded by empty patches of earth overgrown with weeds. Their wooden roofs had crumbled inward long ago. *Farms*, she realized. But the thing that had made her gasp wasn't the number of houses. It was the size of them. They were all—every one of them—built to the scale of mice.

Château Trois Arbres had been the first building she had ever seen that had been made specifically for mice. But this was an entire mouse city, and it had lain abandoned for a hundred years. Delphine's gaze was locked on the sight.

Suddenly she heard Ysabeau's voice behind her. "Bearnois! What's wrong?" The bee was still hovering close to the forest floor, his antennae twitching.

"He won't come up!" Ysabeau continued. She had one of the dried honeysuckle flowers in her paw, but Bearnois wasn't budging. She scampered back down the pile of stone blocks and approached the bee slowly, flower outstretched.

"It's not only Bearnois who feels funny." Alexander leaned close to Delphine. "This place seems . . . strange."

Delphine gazed out again, toward the center of the city. "No," she responded, surprising herself. "It feels like home."

✳ ✳ ✳

After much coaxing, Ysabeau managed to talk Bearnois into joining them inside the city walls. His buzzing was back to its normal hum, but he still seemed on edge.

"I can't figure it out," Ysabeau said. "I can usually read exactly what he's thinking. But all I can tell is that he senses danger of some kind."

Cornichonne nodded solemnly. "I feel the same way."

The little group headed down an overgrown cobblestone path toward the center of the city. Pale stone buildings loomed silently on either side. Ysabeau was in good spirits again, despite her concerns about Bearnois. After all, she had spent so much time in these ruins when she was young, she knew them like the back of her paw. She pointed out architectural details and artistic touches on the buildings as they passed. Delphine lingered on the marks of the rats' destruction: broken front doors, smashed windows, and claw marks everywhere.

They emerged into the central square. Twilight was now deep upon them, but Delphine could still get a sense of how large it was.

"Voilà!" Ysabeau spread her paws. "Isn't it beautiful?"

The buildings along the edges of the city square still retained some of their ornamental filigree. On the ground, flagstones interspersed with lines of black stones led the eye toward the fountain at the center.

They walked across the flagstones. Ysabeau became silent, evidently lost in memory. Delphine could imagine how magical it must have been for her to discover this place as a child.

"You never brought any of your friends here?" Delphine asked. She remembered when she had discovered a hidden room in the snail stables of Château Desjardins as a young mouse; the very first thing she had done was tell Jaq and Gus.

Ysabeau shook her head. "I didn't have a lot of friends growing up." She patted Bearnois as he buzzed alongside her. "It's probably why I'm so good with the royal bees. Back then I spent a lot of time listening to the world around me."

"Why?" Having grown up with an entire château full of extended family members, Delphine found Ysabeau's childhood fascinating.

"We lived in the countryside. Not many other families nearby. It was fine when I was a pinkie mouse, but when I grew up, I wanted the excitement of crowds, conversation, parties. That's one of the reasons I headed to the castle."

Delphine pictured young Ysabeau, kissing her parents good-bye and setting out for adventure. "I can't imagine being that brave," she admitted.

The pawmaid laughed, delighted. "I think you're awfully brave," she replied. "And you know, bravery isn't a lack of fear. It means being afraid, and doing what you have to do anyway."

Delphine laughed, too. "Well, I've been terrified for most

of this trip." She took a little breath. "Less terrified now that you're along, if I'm being honest. Thank you for finding us."

Ysabeau nodded. "Of course."

Bearnois was lagging behind, his buzzing growing more uncertain as they neared the center of the square. Ysabeau glanced back at him.

"Strange. He doesn't want to go near the fountain." She reached out one paw toward the bee, and he twitched his antennae.

Delphine, on the other hand, felt pulled to the old relic. At its center stood the statues of two stone mice holding a spindle between them. Their blank eyes had stared at the empty city for a century.

Delphine recognized them instantly from mouse legends. "Arachne and Rhapso," she breathed.

Alexander got a dreamy look in his eyes. "My hedgehog nannies used to tell me their story—how Arachne spun moonlight into silver thread to save our kingdom. They always said she still watches over us." He gave a little bow to the fountain.

Delphine gazed at the stone figures and the spindle in their paws. Beneath a century of grime, she could see it was gold. She scrambled up onto the edge of the fountain for a better look, ignoring Bearnois's nervous buzzing.

Alexander reached out. "Delfie, watch o—" But he was too late.

Something sharp stabbed deep into the side of her paw. "Ouch!" A long-dead rose vine, thicker than any she had ever seen, was still wound around the base of the fountain. She examined her paw. A huge silver thorn had lodged itself deep in her flesh.

Alexander knelt down. "Allow me." Before she had time to react, he had yanked it out with a single hard pull.

"*Ow!*" Her voice echoed through the courtyard, shattering the silence. It felt like her cry had awoken the city.

Alexander kept her injured paw in his grasp. "Are you all right?"

"I'm fine." She grimaced. It didn't hurt as much now that the thorn was gone. "Talk about a good way to keep the fountain safe."

✳ ✳ ✳

Ysabeau made camp in one of the buildings on the square. Delphine gazed up at the broken skylight above as Cornichonne climbed down through the opening to join them. Smoke from their twigfire spiraled up into the night sky. The old fire pit in the center of the room told Delphine that Ysabeau had often spent the night here.

Ysabeau smiled. "It's nice to be back."

Delphine knew what she meant. She thought again of her initial reaction to seeing the abandoned city . . . of how it had felt like home. Not as if she had actually been to the ruins before, but as if she could imagine what it had been like to live within these walls a hundred years ago. She curled up under Cornichonne's chin. "Will you be warm enough?"

Ysabeau snuggled against Bearnois. He had finally relaxed enough to settle down on the floor for the night, pulling in his little bee knees. "Yes. You can't imagine how cozy it is to curl up with a bumblebee."

Alexander gazed into the flames of the twigfire as he polished his sword. He had that gleam in his eye that he got whenever he was about to launch into one of his tales of derring-do. "Did I ever tell you the story of how I defeated the snake that was terrorizing the farmlands around the castle?"

Delphine smiled softly. "I don't think so."

He wriggled his shoulders, warming to his tale. "Snakes are said to live for centuries, and this one had been around for so long that parents told stories about him to their children at night. He was called Fire-Eye, because his red diamond eyes burned like twin flames.

"Fire-Eye was killing anyone who crossed his path. Nobody could stop him. So one night, I headed to his lair, where a small guardfire burned outside. 'Almighty serpent!' I called. 'Might I hear your tales of bravery?'

"Amused, Fire-Eye slithered toward me as I sat down by the fire. He leered, showing his fangs, but I did not flinch. 'You're quite brave, little mouse,' said he. 'I will share my tales with you.' Story after story he told, and with each one I threw more twigs on the flames.

"Thus it went all night, and the fire grew larger until it roared up to the stars.

"'I see you are the most powerful creature in all the land,' I said to him at last. 'But even you must be afraid of something. That fire, for example. Anyone would fear such a fire.'

"He laughed. 'I can snuff out that fire in an instant.' And he slithered toward the flames that were roaring so high they made my eyes water. He began to coil himself around the fire to put it out, but it was so hot that it overwhelmed him. In an instant, he was burned to a crisp." Alexander chuckled. "And thus ended the reign of Fire-Eye."

Delphine snorted. "If that were really true, the air would have stunk of cooked snake for days."

"Oh, it did," said Alexander quite seriously. But he winked at her as he wrapped himself up in his travel cloak. In an instant, he was softly snoring.

Soon Delphine, too, fell asleep. In her dream, she found herself back at Château Trois Arbres, standing at the window in the hall of tapestries. Rage surged inside her, and she called the blue lightning out of the needle. It was so strong that it burned away the last of the tarnish on the surface. But it was *too* strong. The needle shattered in her paws, and the fragments were carried away on a dark thread of mist. She chased after it, out of the château and through the woods. The mist wreathed upward and formed the shape of her childhood home, Château Desjardins. And then she was standing on the doorstep where she had been found as a baby. A gleaming silver thread led away beneath the door, but when she tried the handle, it was locked tight.

Delphine awoke in a cold sweat. The city lay silent. A pale stream of moonlight was shining through the window. The fire had burned down to embers. Delphine crawled out from Cornichonne's fur, holding her needle sheath, and tiptoed to the door.

Outside, the night air smelled like winter. She walked slowly through the square, gazing around at the buildings that had stood empty for more than a century.

This city was here when the Threaded still existed. The thought sent tingles along her whiskers. Perhaps sparked by her dream, she recalled the tales that Philomène had told her in the hall of tapestries at Château Trois Arbres, how the Threaded had traveled far and wide when they weren't home in their castle in the clouds. Perhaps they had visited this very city.

Standing in the moonlight, she felt a familiar tickle in her paws. The magic was calling her. She gently slid her needle from its sheath.

The flagstones beneath her paws seemed to shudder. She glanced around. Had she imagined that? She rubbed her paws along the engravings on the bright silver needle. In the moonlight, she could see the symbols more clearly than ever before. She turned her needle this way and that, trying to make sense of the intricate loops and whorls.

The stones shuddered again. Something sharp stabbed her paw and she yelped. The sound echoed through the square. She knelt down, pushing aside her petticoats to find another silvery thorn in her paw, this one even larger than the last one. It must have been lying in the dirt between the flagstones. She gritted her teeth and pulled it out swiftly.

The square was silent again. She stood, glancing around. The sense she had felt earlier of familiarity was gone, replaced by the eerie feeling that someone—or something—was watching her. No longer interested in exploring, she retreated to the room where the others lay asleep. Cornichonne snored gently. Delphine curled up against her. She lay awake for a long time, her paw throbbing from the new wound.

Chapter 4

The dead city was even more beautiful in the morning sun. Light streamed across the buildings and sparkled against the frescoes. Ysabeau was already up, sitting on the edge of the fountain and gazing at the square. She looked over when she saw Delphine approach. "All this, untouched for the last hundred years. I used to sit for hours and imagine what life had been like back then."

Delphine sat down next to her. "I've been thinking a lot

about what happened a hundred years ago. That's when my ancestor fled from the rats."

Ysabeau nodded. "I remember. She was carrying a needle of the Threaded."

Of course. Ysabeau had been in Princess Petits-Oiseaux's chambers that day at Château Trois Arbres, when Delphine had told the princess everything she had learned up to that point: her discovery that the needle she had been found with as an orphan was a relic of the Threaded. How she had fled from the rats to Tymbale Monastery and on to Fortencio Academie, learning about her ancestor who had last traveled with the needle. How Delphine had followed in her footsteps in hopes of uncovering more about her mysterious past.

"She was carrying a baby, too," Delphine added.

"But how had she come by the needle in the first place? And who was the baby?" Ysabeau wondered.

Delphine shook her head. "I don't know. I guess the baby could have been my great-great-grandmother? More mysteries I don't have time to solve, not right now." She kicked at the dirt around the fountain, pointedly avoiding the thorny rose vines. "I can't waste time on mice who died a hundred years ago when mice are dying right now." It hurt to dismiss her ancestor like that, but she had to stay focused.

Ysabeau spoke with a gentle voice. "It must be difficult, not knowing the full story."

"Can we go look at the wall of symbols you told me about?" Delphine asked, wanting to change the subject.

Ysabeau's face brightened. "Of course! Follow me." With Bearnois buzzing softly at her side, she led Delphine down a broad street and into a building with a welcoming facade.

"I think this was an inn," Ysabeau said as they picked their way through a crumbling front common room. The ceiling loomed high above them. A staircase at the back of the room led upward, but much of it had rotted away and fallen to the ground. Ysabeau led Delphine to the wall beneath the staircase.

Delphine couldn't believe her eyes. The stones were engraved with swirling runes.

"Those are the symbols on your needle, aren't they?" Ysabeau bounced on her tiptoes.

Delphine withdrew her needle and held it up to compare. Like all the other walls around them, the stones were criss-crossed with the jagged scratches of rat claws, but she could still see enough of the runes to be certain. "Yes. They're the same."

Ysabeau's eyes sparkled. "Exactly?"

"No . . ." Delphine was comparing them more carefully now, one by one. "More like an alphabet. Same symbols, in a different order. But this is still incredible!" She glanced at Ysabeau. "I've never seen anything like these symbols anywhere else, and I've been watching for them my entire life!"

The needle trembled a little as her enthusiasm spilled over

into it, and bits of silvery magic bubbled out. The symbols on the stones flared to life, as if moonlight were flowing through the wall. As the mice watched, three silver lines appeared in a rectangle on the wall, forming the shape of a door around the symbols.

"Is that . . . ?"

The lines were glowing even more brightly than the symbols. Delphine took a step forward, reaching out a paw—

—and a hidden door swung inward, revealing a large, beautiful room.

Daylight streamed through tall windows behind a four-poster bed. Closer to the door sat a table, chairs, and a sofa, all arranged for entertaining. The room was clean and untouched. It had stood awaiting its next guest for the last hundred years.

"The rats didn't know this was here," said Delphine in disbelief.

"Neither did I." Ysabeau's voice was high with excitement. "How did you . . . ?" She was staring at Delphine.

Delphine shrugged, suddenly self-conscious. "I don't know," she admitted. "Half the time that's how the magic works. As if it's deciding what *it* wants to do, not the other way around."

Ysabeau blinked. "Wait. You're not controlling it?"

"No, I am." Delphine struggled to explain. "It's like something is supposed to happen and so I simply . . . let it happen. Almost as if I'm putting my feelings in charge, and they power the magic."

"How strange."

Delphine turned to look back at the door they had come through, and stopped in her tracks. The wall was covered with a beautiful fresco of a sunset. Amber light streamed behind distant mountains. Creamy clouds floated in the sky. And there, resting amid the billows of white, the artist had painted a castle glowing with golden light.

"A castle in the clouds," murmured Delphine. "The home of the Threaded."

Ysabeau wandered through the room, examining everything with burning curiosity. "This is incredible, Delphine. Nothing else in the city is even close to being this well preserved." Bearnois floated along behind her, his dark eyes unreadable. "But why was this room hidden?" Ysabeau mused, peering out of the tall windows.

Delphine tore herself away from the fresco. She looked around at the rest of the room. "For the Threaded." The words flew out of her mouth. "They traveled across the kingdom. The old legends always said so. They would have needed somewhere to stay. If they visited a certain city often enough, maybe they would have their own room waiting for them."

"But why keep it hidden?"

"It wasn't hidden. There were Threaded symbols all over the door, remember?" Her heart thudded as the pieces fell into place. "It was in plain sight. Just locked, so only the Threaded could get in." She ran her paw over the silken coverlet of the bed, admiring the intricate embroidery. A glimmer in the corner of the room caught her eye. She scurried to it and knelt down. There was a tiny fragment of shining silver thread lying in the shadows, as if it had been snipped away from a finished sewing project. Delphine picked it up, and her paw tingled for a moment, like the tingle from the magic of the needle. She slipped the thread fragment into her pocket, feeling a little thrill inside her. She flashed to the days at Château Desjardins not that long ago, when she'd recite her favorite Threaded nursery rhyme to the pinkie mice:

The First rides the wind. The Second walks on light.
The Third bends the waves. The Fourth moves with might.
The Fifth sings with birds. The Sixth paints the sky.
The Seventh writes the song. The Eighth draws the eye.
The Ninth touches stars. The Tenth sweetens tart.
The Eleventh reads the dreams. And the Twelfth knows the heart.

"What's this?" Delphine turned to see Ysabeau standing at a little wooden writing desk next to the bed. As Delphine moved to join her, she spotted a sheaf of papers lying on the dark, glossy surface. The ink on the papers almost looked as if it were still wet.

The two mice spread out the papers on the larger table, admiring the flowery handwriting and bright copper ink. Some pages were covered with words, others with the symbols that had glowed on the wall outside the hidden room. They leaned over the sheets they could read.

"*Thou shalt keep kindness in thy heart,*" read Delphine aloud. "*Thou shalt use thy needle in the service of others.* It's a list of commandments!"

"Like a handbook?"

"Maybe." Delphine kept reading. "*Meddle not with the passage of time. Steal not from coming Death.*" She looked back down at the needle. Her paw was pale from clutching it so tightly. "The needle can do that?"

"It says to *not* do that," Ysabeau pointed out.

But the possibility of learning more about the magic was too exciting for Delphine to ignore. "*The passage of time,*" she repeated. "Does that mean turning back the clock somehow?" Delphine looked out the windows at a dead leaf hanging from a tree. She raised her needle.

Ysabeau narrowed her eyes. "Are you . . . ?"

Ignoring Ysabeau, Delphine willed the withered leaf to return to how it must have looked in summer when it was green and full.

Instead, the needle bucked in her paw and a wave of uneven magic shot across the room, knocking over a chair. The leaf remained brown.

"Delphine, what—" Ysabeau's voice was low.

At that moment, a yowl of pain echoed down the street, high and caustic to their ears.

"Cornichonne!" Delphine snatched up the papers in a crumpled pile, part of her thankful that she didn't have to answer Ysabeau. They dashed from the room and pounded down the street toward the main square. Bearnois raced behind them, buzzing madly.

As they rounded the corner, Delphine gasped, clutching her needle. The rose vine on the fountain had wrapped itself around Cornichonne's paws. She thrashed, howling in pain as the thorns dug into her. Alexander was stabbing fiercely at the vine with his sword.

Delphine's heart raced at the sight of her friend in pain. But instead of fear, she felt anger simmering inside her—anger that once again her friends had been put in danger. She sent a bolt of magic straight into the vine. As if in response, yet another tendril of rose vine unwrapped itself from the fountain base, this time heading straight for Alexander. Delphine screamed and Alexander turned just in time.

"Beetles and boils!" With a sharp thrust of his sword, he sliced back the tendril. Delphine slashed at the vines as well, bright blue magic pouring out of the needle, until the coils loosened. The cat kicked them away weakly.

"Run!" Ysabeau cried. She pointed at the edge of the square, eyes wide. All around them, rose vines were exploding up between the flagstones.

The group turned tail and ran, following Ysabeau. "There's another hole in the wall up ahead!" They rounded a corner, racing past the cottages and farmland on the edge of the city. More and more of the vines were bursting out of the ground behind them.

As they scrambled through the opening, Delphine turned for one last glance back. The vines were still growing, but they weren't reaching out for the mice anymore. They were weaving back and forth on themselves, building another layer of defense around the Dead City.

"Look! I think the city is . . . protecting itself." cried Delphine.

"From what?" asked Alexander, bewildered. "Ysabeau, it never tried to attack you before, did it? What could it have been afraid of?"

Ysabeau shook her head. "I can't imagine."

But Delphine's stomach turned, remembering the needle's jolt in the secret room—right before Cornichonne's cry. It seemed the forbidden spell she'd tried on the dead leaf might have been more powerful than she knew. . . .

interlude

From a little window, Rien watched the mice practicing their magic on the stones outside the fortress. He counted ten of them in the moonlight, all gracefully wielding their needles as they summoned silvery streams of magic. One turned a pebble into a tiny bird that fluttered around her head. Another drew a rainbow through the air.

Two elderly mice stood off to one side. Their voices carried to him on the wind.

"Where are they? We need to get started."

"Patience," replied a mouse with short brown fur. Rien knew that he was the Needle-Master. "They've just returned from Montrenasse. They may be tired from the long journey."

"I don't like it," said the first one. "Rules are rules, and we always gather under the full moon to spin another batch of thread."

The Needle-Master sighed, and Rien could tell he was used to dealing with the nervous fussing of the other one.

Rien turned his attention back to the mice who were practicing. He always took every opportunity to watch them conjure up beauty with their long, silvery needles. He knew that only the chosen twelve were permitted to use the magic, but it was still wonderful to imagine being one of them.

An elegant black mouse appeared from the fortress and darted toward the two elders, needle in one paw. She had her back to Rien, so he couldn't hear what she was saying, but he could see the first mouse scowling even more deeply.

The sound of pawsteps in the stone hallway grabbed Rien's attention. His heart leapt in his chest. He had been waiting for days for Elodie's return.

She dashed into their secret alcove, still wearing her cloak, eyes glowing in excitement. Tossing aside her travel bag, she pulled Rien into a hug. He winced as she squeezed his ribs. He had received a savage beating from the head cook that morning. Luckily, she didn't notice his expression.

"Rien, mon ami, I have such wonderful news! I came straight here to tell you first!"

"What?" He couldn't help but smile. She was like a butterfly flitting around the room. "Did something happen on your trip to the workshop?"

"Oh, Rien, I met the most handsome mouse in the kingdom . . ." Her voice trailed off and her eyes grew dreamy. "He works as a weaver, but he said he would come visit me here sometime." She gazed at Rien. "You'd like him, I'm sure of it."

Rien's heart warmed to see his best friend so happy. Over the years she had become the sister he had never had. "What's his name?" he asked. "Tell me all about him."

"Maturin," said Elodie. She dug around in her pocket and retrieved a paper-wrapped packet. "He gave me some of his favorite treat. I saved it to share with you." She unfolded the paper to reveal a golden chunk of sweet honeycomb.

"You didn't have to do that," insisted Rien, trying to ignore the fragrant scent of the honey. His mouth watered.

"Don't be silly! We share everything." She neatly broke the honeycomb into two pieces and popped her piece into her mouth. "Delicious!"

Rien savored his half, licking the drops of honey off his claws. All too soon it was gone.

"Perhaps we have a courtship on our paws," he teased.

She batted at him. "Silly! Who knows what will happen . . ." But hope shone on her face, making him smile. Everything awful in his life—the beatings, the constant hunger, the bone-chilling cold of the stone room where he slept—it all fell away whenever he was around her. She was a golden sun, spreading happiness, and he drank it up hungrily.

"They say it's lucky to begin a courtship on a full moon," he told her. He had heard the kitchen staff say that many times before.

Elodie's face crumpled. "The full moon! No wonder Gielle was in such a hurry to join the rest!" She pawed at the bag on the floor, tearing it open and pulling out her needle. Rien had only seen it up close a few times. Oversize and silver like the rest, it was dazzling.

"Oh, they'll have my tail on a platter for this! I'll be back soon, I promise!" With a grimace, she flew down the hallway and disappeared.

He returned to the window, sucking the last traces of honey from his paws. Soon Elodie emerged below, dashing to join the rest of the Threaded. They welcomed her into their circle, weaving shimmering magic between their paws and raising their needles to the sky. As the moonlight streamed down, they caught it on their needles and spun it into a strand of delicate silver thread that was so light it floated in the air. Rien remembered the first book that Elodie had helped him read: the story of how Rhapso had taught Arachne to spin moonlight into thread. "This is how the Threaded began," she had told him. "With kindness and knowledge freely given."

Rien leaned against the stone wall as he watched, careful of his bruised ribs. He was so lucky to live here, alongside the Threaded and their beautiful magic. So lucky.

the Laguiole moon

Chapter 5

"Now what?" Alexander paced by the fire, watching as Ysabeau examined Cornichonne's wounds.

Delphine tore her eyes away from the cat to focus on Alexander. "I want to show you what I found in the Dead City."

"Was it something to do with the runes Ysabeau mentioned?"

She nodded, pulling the crumpled sheets of paper out of her pocket. Alexander gently took them, smoothing out the creases with his paws.

"These look ancient. Why are they all wadded up like this?" His eyes narrowed. "Did—did you do this? Old papers should be treated with care. I once found a crumbling vellum scroll in the Forbidden Wing, and when I took it to the castle librarians, they were impressed with how carefully I had transported—"

"Alexander. The point is that the symbols from my needle were carved into a wall, exactly as Ysabeau described. I opened a magical door in that wall and discovered a room that was just for the Threaded. That's where we found these."

He scanned the papers quietly. Ysabeau started brushing the cat with a dried thistle. Bearnois perched nearby, waiting for his turn to be brushed. Alexander looked up at Delphine. "These look like rules. Did you read these?"

"Some of them. I was a little distracted." Another pang of guilt swept across her at the sight of Cornichonne licking her wounds as Ysabeau continued to brush her fur. Delphine shoved it down deep and squared her shoulders. "But if there were rules that the Threaded had to follow—"

"Probably for a good reason—"

Delphine pretended not to hear. "—then we have proof that the needles held tremendous power. Which is what I'll need in order to defeat Midnight. *Real* power, like the kind I summoned that night at Château Trois Arbres. I have to figure out how to do that again, when the time comes."

"Delfie. I saw you that night. You . . . you frightened me. Don't you remember?"

Delphine recalled how the needle had spattered angry sparks in every direction, burning holes in the carpet and the skirts of her gown. How the needle had felt ice-cold against her paws, not warm as it usually did. How the screams coming from other parts of the château had filled her with hatred for the rats, and then despair at being unable to save any of the victims. "I remember."

"Then you know why that's a bad road to go down. There has to be another way to defeat him."

She gritted her teeth. "I don't have time to figure out another way. His minions are out there right now, laying waste to the kingdom." Taking the papers, she stalked off.

"I believe in you!" he called after her, but she kept walking. In some tiny part of her heart, she hoped he would follow. She *needed* him to follow. But he stayed where he was.

Outside of camp, Delphine found a patch of dry moss and sank down in a heap. What was she going to do? She flipped through the pages, reading the parts that were legible. The moral code at the beginning gave way to Threaded anecdotes of bravery and daring. She found it fascinating. Perhaps it was a sort of journal, kept by Threaded guests passing through the inn. But the handwriting was all the same. Maybe one of the Threaded had been documenting their history? She read on, hoping to find a reference to her ancestor. But there was nothing at all about a mouse fleeing with a baby.

When she reached a mention of "a castle that rests atop

clouds," she stopped short. Castles on clouds again. This was more than a coincidence. The former home of the Threaded had to be out there somewhere, even if it lay in ruins; perhaps it held the answers she sought about her ancestor. But right now, the welfare of the kingdom had to come first. Sighing, Delphine rolled up the papers, slid them into her needle sheath around the needle, and headed back to camp.

She found Ysabeau mixing a dandelion-root poultice for Cornichonne's wounds. Alexander was perched on a stump, industriously but ineffectually trying to braid together some long fur strands that Ysabeau had brushed out of Cornichonne's tail. He was deep in concentration but clearly had no idea at all what he was doing.

She peered over his shoulder. "That's the most interesting braid I've ever seen," she said quietly. He jumped, then realized it was Delphine and began to laugh in relief.

"I thought you were a—"

"—hawkworm?" Delphine grinned, glad to feel the frostiness from their previous exchange melting away. "Not quite. But I can help with that . . . if you like."

"Yes, please!" He handed her the hanks of fur.

She set to work with practiced ease. "What are you trying to make, anyway?" she asked as she showed him how to braid.

"Better straps for Cornichonne's travel bags. The ones we made from petticoat fabric are already worn through."

Delphine hadn't even noticed. How distracted with her own

problems had she been over the past few days? She finished braiding the strands, and Alexander watched as she knotted the ends around themselves to create a smooth finish.

"That's magic!" he crowed.

Delphine couldn't help but smirk. "No." She pointed her needle at Alexander. With a silvery burst of sparkles, his whiskers were perfectly curled. "*That's* magic."

"I like that look," Cornichonne whuffled weakly. "Alexander, you should do your whiskers like that all the time."

He felt the curls with amazement. "You didn't tell me you could do that!"

Delphine shrugged and smiled as she resheathed her needle. "Do we need more kindling?" She circled the edges of the campsite, picking up twigs.

"Delfie!" He trotted along behind her. "I've had to do my whiskers on my own, every morning, for this entire trip, and all this time you could have styled them with a wave of your wand?"

"*Needle*, Alexander," she said as she stooped to retrieve another twig. But she couldn't help blushing a little with pride.

In the morning, Cornichonne was back to her spry self, on the hunt for breakfast bugs in the trees near their camp.

"She should be fine now," Ysabeau said, and relief washed over Delphine. "But we're nearly out of food, and I can't forage enough for three of us in the dead of winter. I was barely able to sustain myself during the trek from the château to find you."

Delphine wished yet again that the magic of the needle could create food out of thin air. Summoning wildflowers and lightning bolts didn't make much of a difference when stomachs were growling.

Ysabeau stood and stretched, clearly trying to put on a good face. "We'll head toward the nearest village. It's not too far."

They struck north in the early-morning light. It had snowed again the night before, but only a few flakes had managed to squeeze between the dense pine branches. The ground remained largely bare. Cornichonne walked slowly but evenly, Bearnois floating beside her as they traveled.

After a while, Delphine noticed that the bee's buzzing had taken on a pattern, more like a signal than merely a comforting hum. She looked at Ysabeau. "Does he sense something?"

Ysabeau nodded. She was watching Bearnois carefully. "Strangers up ahead," she replied. "He doesn't think they're a threat, but we should still proceed with care."

Shortly thereafter, they began to hear quiet voices floating through the trees. A child's laugh was cut off sharply, as if shushed by a nervous parent. Someone was singing a lullaby in a low baritone. They approached slowly, ready to turn tail and flee at the first sight of danger.

"Who goes there?" An exhausted-looking mouse stepped out from behind a tree, armed only with a farmer's pitchfork. His simple clothing was torn and dirty. Despite the fear in his eyes, he stood his ground.

Delphine stepped forward. "We're friends," she said. "Just passing through, on our way to . . ." She turned to Ysabeau, realizing she didn't know the name of the village. Then she noticed that Cornichonne had melted away into the trees. The cat must have disappeared so as not to alarm this stranger.

"Soleil-sur-Nieges," responded Ysabeau. "We would pass and continue onward in search of food and supplies, if you will let us."

But the mouse shivered at the name of the village. "Soleil-sur-Nieges is no more."

CHAPTER 6

The farmer mouse led them through the trees, walking quickly but not very expertly. Even Delphine could tell he had never spent time in a dense forest like this one. She kept searching for a glimpse of Cornichonne following along, but the cat had vanished. Delphine had to trust she was fine for now.

Soon they arrived at the perimeter of a makeshift camp in a large clearing. They passed between more farmers who stood as guards, clutching scythes or pitchforks for weapons, and emerged to see a cluster of field mice in thick homespun clothing. The strange mice were huddled around a small fire. It was more smoke than flame, and the pinkie mice kept coughing, but the adults all seemed too exhausted to care. Several had bandaged limbs or tails.

Delphine passed a paw over her eyes. "You were attacked, weren't you?"

"Rats." The farmer's voice was strained. He turned and spoke to the mice around the fire. "These travelers wish us no harm. Shall we let them break bread with us tonight?"

Several assented. The rest seemed past caring. Delphine could see deep shadows beneath their eyes. She approached the fire and sat down next to one of them about her age.

"The rats came," said Delphine gently. "They destroyed your homes, didn't they? And you all fled?" The field mouse nodded, her whiskers drooping low. "Do you know where you're going?"

Another mouse nearby spoke up. Her whiskers hung limp with exhaustion, too, but her eyes were still sharp. "No, but that won't stop us from moving onward until we find safety." She peered at Delphine through the smoke, her blue cap pulled down over her brow. "Our village is—was—outside Montrenasse-sur-Terre. Not much left of it now, after Lymon's band of bruisers tore it apart. Simply means we'll need to build a new town, a better one." She made Delphine think of her mother, never backing down from a challenge. And why did that name, Montrenasse-sur-Terre, sound so familiar?

Delphine's heart broke for these mice, caught in the middle of a war they couldn't have seen coming. "Is there anything we can do to help?" she asked. She hesitated, suddenly realizing how presumptuous she must sound. What help could they possibly offer?

But the mouse in the blue cap nodded. "I don't suppose you have knowledge of what is edible in these woods?"

Ysabeau was glad to offer a lesson on foraging. Within minutes, she had disappeared into the trees with several field mice in tow, all eager to learn. Bearnois floated along with them, always at his mistress's side.

Delphine addressed the mouse in the blue cap. "Is there anything else you need help with?"

She was met with a firm gaze. "If you're not afraid of sorrow, you can assist in comforting those still in shock."

Delphine nodded. Then, with the words *Montrenasse-sur-Terre* still rattling around inside her head, she sat bolt upright. "Oh!" she squeaked. "Philomène!"

"Pardon?" The mouse in the blue cap gave her an odd look.

"You said you lived near Montrenasse-sur-Terre? Do you know if there's still a tapestry workshop there?" Delphine had just remembered the conversation with Philomène. The ancient noblemouse had told her that Montrenasse-sur-Terre once held a workshop where all the Threaded tapestries were woven.

The mouse shrugged. "Never been much for tapestries. And all Montrenasse is likely overrun with rats by now." She looked closely at Delphine. "Get some food in you, it'll calm the nerves." She retrieved an acorn-cap full of weak broth for Delphine, then excused herself. Delphine watched as she crossed to the edge of the clearing and knelt down by a large bundle of fabric, pain etched deep in her face.

Delphine sipped the broth. It was thin, but it still brought strength back into her limbs. *Montrenasse-sur-Terre is nearby,* she thought, trying not to get too distracted from her main quest. Right now this detail was nothing but a useful piece of information to store alongside everything else she had learned about the legendary mice. There would be time in the future to worry about all that. At least, she hoped there would be.

When she had finished the broth, she slowly made her way through the camp, greeting those who spoke to her and repeating her thanks for their hospitality. She longed to provide the companionship that the mouse in the blue cap had said was needed, but what could she do to comfort these refugees? They had lost everything but their lives.

One mouse frowned at her. Tall and gaunt, covered in dappled fur, he seemed to carry the weight of everyone's sorrow on his shoulders.

"Why are you here?" he asked as she drew near. His paws trembled.

"Please." Delphine pointed across the camp at the mouse in the blue cap. "She said you all might like to have some company for a while."

His expression changed. "Flore? She's our leader." He beckoned and Delphine drew closer. "My name is Blé. I'm Flore's second-in-command. Ever since the rat attack, that is." As he said those words, his paws trembled even more.

"I'm Delphine." The pain in Blé's eyes made Delphine want to cry. Suddenly she recalled how Cornichonne's purring had helped her sleep on some of her most restless nights. She spoke impulsively. "Blé—I'm traveling with a friend who might be able to comfort you more than I can."

Blé cast a glance over at Alexander, who was holding court with a ragtag group of young mice hanging on his every word. "Him?"

"No . . ." Delphine bit her lip and thought of Cornichonne, alone out there somewhere in the black forest. She had to try. After all, she and Alexander had overcome their fear of the cat. And so had Ysabeau. Perhaps these mice could as well. "My friend is still in the woods. She didn't want to frighten any of you."

His eyes narrowed. "What kind of mouse could be so frightening?"

"Well . . ." Delphine gulped. "She's actually not a mouse, per se."

His expression hardened. "A rat?!"

"No! Rats are monsters, every last one of them. In fact, I'm trying to find the leader of the rats so that I can stop them for good."

"You?" He looked her up and down, doubt writ large on his face.

She nodded, determined. "Yes, and I won't stop until I succeed."

He gave a bitter laugh. "They say the leader of the rats is as big as a fox. They say he keeps himself hidden away in his lair atop a mountain somewhere. They say he can't die. And *you're* going to stop him?"

Delphine gulped. For the thousandth time, she wondered what exactly she was getting herself into . . . but she wasn't one to back down. She stood up straighter.

"I have a weapon, a magic needle—one of the Threaded's needles. Do you know the stories of the Threaded? They could do all sorts of magic." She felt like she was babbling, but she kept going, hoping to win Blé back from his stony silence. "Look, isn't it beautiful?" She pulled the needle from its golden sheath. The strange symbols shimmered in the pale afternoon light.

Blé froze. "The needle . . . is real?!" He extended one trembling paw to touch the metal shaft. "We've started hearing tales, but we didn't know what to believe. A mouse with magic after all these years . . ."

Delphine had no idea what he was talking about, but she

supposed she *was* a mouse with magic. If that was what she needed to persuade him that Cornichonne was trustworthy, she would be happy to oblige. She gave a little flick of the needle and a snow-white flower bloomed into existence on the icy ground. She heard Blé gasp.

He clutched his paws together as if he had been visited by the gods. "Bring your friend."

Delphine nodded and tiptoed backward, suddenly a bit nervous at his rapture.

She found Cornichonne asleep a little way into the woods. When she woke her to tell her the good news, she could see the relief in the cat's eyes.

"I was worried maybe you would decide that mice were better travel companions for you than a cat," Cornichonne admitted.

"Pish-posh. You're the best companion I could ever hope for."

The cat grinned and followed her back toward the camp.

"But . . . please don't lick your lips in front of them, at least not right away," Delphine said before they stepped into the clearing.

"Promise," said Cornichonne.

When they reentered the camp, Blé was on the other side of the fire, talking to Flore with great excitement. Alexander approached the scene as more mice crowded around. As Delphine emerged with Cornichonne, they all turned to stare, wide-eyed.

"Don't be alarmed," Delphine hastened to say.

But the mice weren't looking at the cat. They were all gazing at Delphine and her needle. A rustling whisper grew among the group. Flore gestured for silence and threaded her way between the mice until she stood before Delphine. She reached out one paw and touched the needle with wonder.

"Are you The One? You must be, if you can tame a . . . what *is* that?" Flore gazed at Cornichonne.

"She's a cat. And actually—" began Delphine, but Flore cut her off.

"So you truly are the Savior of the Needle?" Her voice was thick with hope.

"Um . . ." Delphine had no idea how to answer. Then she caught sight of Alexander standing off to the side, nodding fervently. She stared back into Flore's eyes as firmly as she could. "Yes. Yes, I am."

A cheer of hope erupted from the crowd. Without even giving Cornichonne a second look, Flore swooped up Delphine in a massive hug, lifting her from the ground. Mice ran toward Delphine, reaching out to touch her whiskers, her paws, her cloak. But more than anything to touch the needle. They laid their paws on its silvery surface, timidly at first, then with more and more trust. It was clear they were desperate for something to believe in.

A few of them sidled close to Cornichonne, twisting their

paws. Cornichonne lay down and the littlest children came racing over to climb onto her back. She sniffed at them with her funny, flat nose and they giggled in delight.

Mugs filled with frothy milkwort wine were passed among the crowd. Delphine took an experimental gulp and sneezed as bubbles went straight up her nose. She felt someone slap her good-naturedly on the back and turned to find Alexander, chuckling at her as he took a drink.

"That's half the fun of milkwort wine!" he said, sneezing and laughing at the same time.

"You sound like Cornichonne." Delphine giggled. She took a longer draft and sneezed several times, laughing uncontrollably as she did so.

More wood was heaped onto the fire and it crackled with life. Mice began dancing an enthusiastic branle around the flames. A lanky young farmer mouse in tight trousers seized Delphine by the paw and pulled her into the circle of dancers. She gripped Alexander's shirt with her other paw, and he followed along behind her. As he danced, he leapt into cabriole after cabriole, and all the mice cheered at his elegance. Ysabeau joined the circle, dancing with the grace of a royal lady.

Delphine let herself forget about her worries for the moment. She danced, giggling, feeling the milkwort froth on her lips. Then she noticed an abandoned mug sitting on the ground, still full of milkwort wine. Cornichonne was leaning in with curiosity, taking a sip of the contents.

"Alexander!" Delphine grabbed his wrist, pointing. The cat lifted her head, wrinkling her nose. He and Delphine dove to the ground, and not a moment too soon. Cornichonne reared back and sneezed a cat-size sneeze that sprayed the entire group.

There was a moment of silence as all the field mice stood frozen in shock, bits of cat drool dripping from their clothes and fur. The only sound was the crackling of the fire.

Then, "This is tasty," said Cornichonne before dipping her head back down for a second slurp.

"No!" Alexander and Delphine ran toward the cat, getting there just in time.

"Hang on, Cornichonne," said Delphine, carrying the mug toward the edge of the trees. "Do us a favor and face away from the camp when you drink it, please?"

The cat shrugged, making the fur all along her back ripple in a wave. "All right. But I thought you liked my sneezes?"

Delphine laughed and hugged Cornichonne tight. "I love your sneezes. But our hosts . . ." They turned together to look back at the mice around the campfire. The surprise had subsided, and they were laughing as they wiped cat drool off one another, but Cornichonne got the point.

"Hmm," the cat said, reaching her tongue back down into the mug. "Delfie. I've never met anyone as kind as you."

Delphine felt love bubble up inside her.

Alexander took her paw. "It's true, Delfie. It's an honor to be on this adventure with you."

Her heart grew even more full. Without stopping to think, she wrapped her arms around his neck and planted a kiss on his furry cheek.

He pulled back and blushed, his whiskers quivering. "My lady!"

"What?" She was laughing, but then she caught sight of the look on his face. *Oh no.* She had embarrassed him. She hadn't meant it like that . . . well, not *really.* But then again, it had been nice. Nicer than she wanted to admit. She waved her paw in the air. "Must be the milkwort wine," she said as lightly as she could.

His ears remained pink, but he laughed it off as well. Leaving the cat to her drink, Delphine and Alexander found a log where they could sit and watch the field mice still carousing. It was pleasant to relax and sip their milkwort wine, enjoying each other's company.

"Do you know why they were calling you the savior?" Alexander said finally.

"It's odd, isn't it?"

"I asked. Apparently, word has been spreading that a mouse with a magic needle has come to defeat the rats and save us all." He gave her a sideways glance.

"Oh?" Delphine tipped back her mug and took a gulp big enough to ensure it triggered a sneeze. She didn't want the fun to end, not yet. Alexander chuckled, but then sighed and gently took her paw in his own.

"It's good that they believe in you," he said. "It gives them hope."

Delphine scuffed at the icy ground with the toe of her thin slipper. The faith of all these villagers weighed heavy on her shoulders. And how many more out there were counting on her? "I'm only a simple château mouse," she whispered, her throat dry. "I'm not a legend."

"Every legend was started by a real mouse, once upon a time." He took her mug and placed it on the ground so he could hold both of her paws in his.

She leaned forward and let herself rest her forehead on his shoulder. He smelled of pine sap, and woodsmoke, and, very faintly, of the violet cologne he had worn at the castle, so long ago. She breathed in the smell of Alexander and let it linger.

"I'm afraid," she whispered, so quietly that she wasn't sure if he would hear her.

He pressed his lips to the top of her head. "It's all right to be afraid," he said, his breath tickling her fur. "Fear makes us stronger."

She let out a little laugh. "My mother used to say that."

"You'll hear her say it again," he promised. He wrapped his arms around her, pulling her in close. "You're already the strongest mouse I've ever known."

She was so surprised by this statement that she leaned back to look him in the eyes. "Do you mean that?"

"Hmm?" He raised his eyebrows, then picked up his mug of milkwort wine and took a long, deep gulp. His other arm was still firmly around her, holding her tightly in place.

"No!" she shrieked in delighted terror, and broke away from him to run back toward the campfire. She could hear him running behind her.

"Hang on, Delfie!" He sneezed loudly. "I want to tell you something!" Another sneeze.

She ran toward Cornichonne, who was now lying down with a pile of pinkie mice clambering all over her. "I'll get Cornichonne to sneeze on you!" she cried.

But Alexander merely leaned in and gave a nice big milkwort sneeze right in Delphine's face.

"Eww!" cried the pinkie mice in delighted disgust. Alexander grinned and swaggered away, leaving Delphine to wipe her face with the edge of her skirts.

✳   ✳   ✳

The celebration had died down, and the camp was preparing for dinner. Ysabeau and her erstwhile students had foraged a bounty of roots and winter onions they were gnawing into chunks for a stew.

Delphine led Cornichonne over to Blé. "When I'm tired or sore, I curl up next to her and her purring always makes me feel better. I thought perhaps it might help all of you. . . ."

Blé looked at the cat. Delphine could tell fear and hope were warring inside him. But hope won out. As the cat lay down, he helped the tired mice curl up alongside her. She began to purr, and Delphine watched their faces relax. It was working.

Blé touched his brow. "Thank you," he said. "Never would have guessed a cat could help us mice."

As Delphine made her way back toward the campfire, she spotted some threadbare sacks that needed patching. She sighed with relief—finally, something *she* could do to help. With a borrowed mouse needle and thread, she stitched, listening to snatches of conversations around her. A few mice were discussing the human prince, and Delphine pricked up her ears. Had he finally found his mystery princess?

"It's true love, they say. Can you imagine?" The speaker was bubbling with enthusiasm. "When was the last time a human prince in our kingdom found love?"

The other mouse pursed her lips, clearly less excited about the news. "All the humans have been celebrating for months."

Delphine was about to interrupt and ask for more details, but the second mouse was still talking, her voice tight and hard. "They celebrate while we're being hunted. Humans never have any idea what's happening with the animal citizens of the kingdom. We could all be dead by the next moon and they'd still be singing and dancing about their new princess."

Suddenly Delphine didn't want to listen anymore. She noticed Flore approaching and waved, eager for a distraction.

But as Flore drew closer, Delphine could see something was very wrong.

Flore wasted no time. "We're honored to have you here, Savior." (Delphine flinched a little at the title, but tried not to show it.) "You've already brought comfort to our most exhausted and shown us so much kindness." She twisted her apron between her paws. "I hate to ask, but . . . do you have one more favor left in you?"

She led Delphine to a large bundle of fabric lying on the ground by the fire. Delphine recognized it as the bundle that Flore had been hovering around all afternoon, and she could see now that it was resting on a human playing card so it could be easily carried from place to place.

Flore spoke in a lower voice. "When the rats attacked, one mouse was injured worse than the rest." She knelt next to the bundle and gently lifted the fabric to reveal a mouse no older than Delphine. Pale and wan, he was curled into a ball. Rough bandages encircled his torso.

"My son, Louis. Nothing has helped him, not even our prayers to Arachne and Rhapso."

His eyes were clouded, his nose dry and cracked. At the sound of her voice, his whiskers trembled. "Mother? Are you there?" His voice came in shallow gasps. It was obvious that he was near death.

Flore stared at Delphine, tears spilling down her cheeks.

"Please, Savior. Use the power of your needle to heal him."

KING MIDNIGHT SNARLED IN RAGE, tempted to smash the windows of his throne room just to prove a point. But he had done that before, and it was always more trouble than it was worth. So instead he lashed out with a backhanded blow at the soldier before him.

"What do you mean, *it's gone again?*" he growled. "You couldn't capture one little mouse? You couldn't even steal the needle away from her? What exactly *were* you idiots doing at Château Trois Arbres, having a picnic?!"

The soldier stiffened, bracing himself for another blow, but King Midnight turned away. He couldn't be bothered to waste any more time on this idiot rat. He swept past his head guard, Mezzo, and out of the throne room, doing his best to hide the limp that had plagued him for weeks. His whole body ached, but the worst pains were along the rough scars that crisscrossed his face and chest. He felt certain the twelfth needle would be his salvation, the key to recharging the magic that held him together—but not one of his troops seemed able to find it.

At least Commandant Robeaux had taken some initiative, spreading the word that the treaty had ended. Perhaps he would reward Robeaux. Or perhaps not. Right now, he didn't feel like rewarding anyone for anything.

He stormed through the halls, spittle foaming at the corners of his mouth. He was tired of sitting on his throne, tired of waiting for his troops to report to him. All they brought were excuses.

He found Valentine right where he had expected the ermine would be, in the fortress library. She was the only one who ever bothered to go inside. The ancient books were covered with cobwebs and caked with mildew. But sure enough, there she was, curled up comfortably atop a pile of old leather-bound books, leafing through the onionskin pages of another oversize tome.

"Valentine!" he roared.

The ermine yawned, then unfurled herself and sallied toward him. Her snowy tail twitched lazily.

"Valentine," he said again, when she was finally at his side. "You failed me once before when you let that cursed mouse slip through your paws. This is your second chance."

"*Snurleau* failed you," she purred. "He's a terrible fighter. Couldn't even stand up to two mice." She made a point of looking around the library. "Speaking of the stoat . . . I haven't smelled his hideous odor in quite some time. Did you send him back out on another mission?" She stared at him, and her unblinking eyes were far too bright.

"I grew tired of him." Midnight stared back at her with a dangerous smile, picturing how Snurleau had slumped to the floor of the throne room after he buried that dagger in the stoat's chest. "Now did you hear what I said? Get that mouse or you won't work for me anymore!"

"Oh, *King* Midnight," she said, her voice as sharp as a steel blade. "I work for you because I enjoy it. Not because I have to." She slithered through the door and was gone down the hallway before he could think of a response.

Midnight roared, a terrible sound that echoed down the empty hallways. He took a step forward and his bad leg buckled beneath him.

Chapter 7

Delphine scrambled backward on the frozen ground, desperate to escape the smell of blood. The faces of the slain at the château swam up before her eyes. She stared frantically at Flore. "I can't help him!"

"Yes you can." Flore's faith was unwavering, far beyond any level of faith Delphine had ever had in anything in this world. "We have heard of what you can do. You can save Louis, heal him where the rats tore his belly open." She reached for Delphine. "I believe."

The other mice were slowly encircling them, heads bowed, all whispering "I believe." *I believe, I believe, I believe.* It echoed through Delphine's entire body. She took a deep breath. Who knew what the magic might be capable of? Slowly she reached back to unsheathe her needle, only to feel a firm grasp on her paw.

"Delfie," Alexander whispered in her ear. "This is wrong. Can't you sense it?"

She shook her head, trying to ignore him. She couldn't listen to him, couldn't listen to anything if she had any hope of succeeding.

But Alexander continued, more urgently. "The papers from the Dead City, Delfie. They said not to cheat Death, remember? *'Steal not from coming Death'?* This is what it was talking about. *Delfie!*"

She pushed Alexander's paw away and pulled out the needle from its sheath. It was already glowing in her grasp. She gazed at Louis's crumpled face and milky eyes. She could tell his wound was still bleeding from the stains on the bandages. She knew what happened when a mouse was injured this badly. Everyone knew. But she had to try.

Delphine pointed the needle toward him as he lay swaddled in the makeshift blankets. She tried to relax but fear pounded through her, making her paws shake. With a deep breath, she demanded that the silvery sparkles make themselves known.

Nothing. She grew angry at herself and how she had so blithely summoned a flower out of the ice earlier in the day. *Useless,* she told herself, *everything you do with your magic is useless.* The rats had hurt this poor mouse. It was up to her to make it right.

Her anger took form and rushed with painful pinpricks through her paws, pouring from her needle onto Louis's body in a torrent of cold blue magic. But he remained unchanged. She redoubled her efforts, trying to bring him back from the brink. Somehow she could *feel* the wound inside him, but it was just out of reach. The fear of failure swirled around her, overwhelming her, and the connection was broken. The needle lay dead in her paws. Louis's wound bled on, his chest rising and falling in short, shallow pants.

Flore gave a little squeak. It cut Delphine to the quick. She clenched the needle, pleading with it to come back to life, trying to force more magic out of it by sheer determination. There was a painful tug inside her, as if the needle were yanking her last drop of energy from her, and then the needle went ice-cold. She felt suddenly drained.

"I'm sorry," she muttered. "I don't know how to . . ."

Then Alexander and Ysabeau were there, their arms protectively around her. "You did everything you could," whispered

Ysabeau, and Alexander nodded. Delphine let herself lean on Alexander. She was so tired.

"I tried." The words felt pointless, but she kept saying them, trying to convince herself that it was true. "I tried."

Flore, still hunched over Louis, nodded each time Delphine said it, as if it were some kind of charm. "You did, you did," she kept repeating, with increasing fervency. She lifted her head, her eyes hot. "I believe in you, Savior of the Needle," she said. Her voice was hoarse. "I believe in you. I believe you *did* help him. Look!" She cupped his pale face in her paws. "He's getting better, I'm sure of it!"

Delphine shook her head. She could see that nothing had changed, that Louis was still at death's door.

But Flore wasn't paying attention to Delphine anymore. She was entreating the other mice, more and more loudly, to come confirm that Louis looked better. They leaned over nervously, murmuring uncertain responses beneath their breaths. Nobody wanted to be the one to point out that Louis did not look better at all.

Alexander and Ysabeau tiptoed backward, taking Delphine with them. They retreated to where Cornichonne and Bearnois were curled up with the sleeping mice, and found an empty spot next to Cornichonne's head.

Delphine couldn't bear to sit, not when she could still hear Flore repeating her son's name over and over. But Alexander pulled her gently downward, and she was too tired to resist. He slipped off her needle sheath and tucked her in beneath Cornichonne's chin.

"Sleep, Delfie," he said. He curled up alongside her. She lay in the dark, trying to see the moon through the trees. What had happened? Why hadn't she been able to heal Louis? *I'm still not strong enough*, she thought as she drifted off into a restless sleep.

The camp was just waking up when a keening cry broke through the icy morning air. Delphine leapt up. The wail came again, from the direction of the campfire. She swung her sheath onto her back and yanked out her needle, running as fast as she could. Were the rats attacking?

What she saw stopped her dead in her tracks. Flore, wailing uncontrollably, clutched her son's cold body in her arms.

"What happened?" Blé shoved his way through the crowd. Everyone else was standing silent, brokenhearted for Flore. Blé knelt down, feeling Louis's neck, then shook his head slowly. "Flore. When did this happen?"

Flore was too overcome to talk. She rocked back and forth, squeezing her bundle as if she could bring her son back to life by sheer force of will.

Delphine's heart clenched. She took a step forward.

"Flore . . . I am so sorry. I wish I could have saved him. I thought—"

Flore's head hung limp over Louis's body. She said nothing.

Blé's gaze shot upward. His eyes burned holes into Delphine. "You did this."

"No," she whispered, but her voice trembled. Her paw opened of its own accord. The needle hit the ground with a thud.

Blé was ablaze with anger. "This is your fault! You're the reason he died!" Next to him, Flore shook silently.

Delphine shrank back. Her paws were freezing cold. They didn't even feel like her own paws.

Ysabeau and Alexander stepped protectively in front of Delphine, shielding her from Blé. "He was already dying!" cried Alexander. "We all saw him last night, how he could barely breathe. It would have happened no matter what Delphine did!"

Blé was holding Flore against him as she wept. "Traitor!" he spat at Delphine. "You're not The One. You're nothing. You lied!"

More and more accusations were being lobbed from all sides. "How did you get that needle?" "Where is the true savior?" "What did you do to her?"

Delphine stumbled backward, tripping on a root. She nearly fell, but Alexander grabbed her arm. Ysabeau remained rigid and defiant in front of her, protecting her from the mob that was forming.

Flore rose to stand in the center of the group, tears still streaming. "*Liar!*" Her broken voice cut through the din of screeching mice. "You stole the savior's needle. You took her name. You have no place here among us!" The declaration hung in the air.

All the other mice took it up, crying it out as well. "Liar! Liar!" They reached out toward her, hungry for vengeance.

Delphine ran, not caring that she had left her needle lying on the frozen earth. She could hear Alexander and Ysabeau running behind her. Tears stung her eyes as she pictured Louis's lifeless body. The pain she had seen on Flore's face tore Delphine to shreds. She had done her best to save Louis. How could the field mice turn on her like that? Her throat tightened.

She heard Alexander and Ysabeau calling out behind her. "Delphine! Calm down, Delphine, they're not following us!"

She let herself slow to a walk, then realized with horror they had left Cornichonne behind. She clenched her paws. Couldn't she do anything right? She spun to face them. "We have to go back for Cornichonne!"

"Cornichonne's on her way," replied Ysabeau. "Bearnois told her it was time to go." She gently placed the needle in Delphine's paw. "You would have regretted leaving this behind."

"I should have tried harder." Bitterness made Delphine's chest hurt. "I failed them."

Alexander placed an arm around Delphine's shoulders to pull her in for a hug, but she shrugged it off. He put his paws up.

"They shouldn't have asked you in the first place. It wasn't fair of them to expect you to do the impossible."

"That's the thing, Alexander!" Delphine knew she was growing frantic, but she couldn't stop herself. "It's *not* impossible! Don't you see? The simple fact that the papers from the Dead City warned against it means it *can* be done! There's so much more to the needle's magic, if I could only figure out how to reach it!"

Alexander crossed his arms. "You already know how to do a great deal with the needle."

"I don't know *anything*. I can summon flowers and melt ice. I am completely in the dark on how to summon its *true* power, and I have to somehow stop a rat that is apparently the size of a fox and can't die. What am I going to do? Stitch him a giant cape of flowers?"

"That's not what Alexander is saying," Ysabeau replied in her gentle voice.

At that moment, Cornichonne and Bearnois emerged from the trees. Delphine looked at the cat. Cornichonne still loved her. Cornichonne believed in her.

The cat looked back at Delphine. "Listen to them," she said in her low, raspy voice. "They're right."

"Oh, nutmegs to all of you!" Delphine shoved her needle back into its sheath. "I'm going to find a place to curl up and get some more sleep. You can all join me when you jolly well please." She turned and stomped away into the forest.

Eventually, she found a clearing large enough for a makeshift campsite, littered with plenty of dead leaves. She pulled out her needle to swirl the leaves into squishy bed piles, but her paws were still shaking and the magic sputtered. She was too tired to care. She clambered into a half-gathered pile to wait for the others.

Her mind kept going back to the look on Louis's face the night before, just before she had lost her connection with the magic. Had it been her imagination, or had his eyes begun to glow blue? Had she felt his body beginning to heal? Or was that merely wishful thinking?

Worst of all, what if the papers of the Threaded were right and she should never have tried to defeat Death in the first place? She thought about the Dead City's reaction to her attempt to bring the leaf back to life. Delphine shuddered, knowing that her chill had nothing to do with the frozen ground. She curled her tail around her ankles and stared up at the sky.

The next day, they trudged in silence through the forest, Ysabeau up front and Alexander taking the rear. Delphine could feel Alexander's eyes on her. Finally, she couldn't take it any longer. "Alexander? What do you want to say?"

He was quiet for a while. Then he cleared his throat. "That's exactly the sort of thing I was afraid was going to happen."

"What sort of thing?" Delphine could tell Ysabeau and Cornichonne were listening up ahead, but she didn't care. They weren't the ones who had to save an entire kingdom.

"Maybe the magic of the needle isn't intended for all purposes." She knew what his face would look like if she glanced at him. Worried, beseeching, his big eyes full of sympathy. She didn't turn around. "You're letting fear of failure overtake you, and it's starting to push you to try magic you shouldn't."

"That wasn't the problem!" Delphine's nostrils flared. Alexander was supposed to stand by her, no matter what. "The problem was that I didn't go far *enough*! Didn't try hard enough! I could have saved him!"

But Alexander didn't budge. "You showed those ancient papers to me," he replied. "And then you did exactly what they warned against. You knew in your heart it was wrong to try, and that made you afraid, and the fear undermined you. The fear drained all your power. We watched it happen."

"Well, it doesn't matter, does it, because I wasn't able to save him anyway," she shot back. The wind was picking up, cutting through the branches and slipping inside their makeshift cloaks. She shivered, unable to get Louis's face out of her mind.

"You *couldn't* have saved him." He tried to catch her gaze. "Delfie, you're not listening to me. It wasn't your fault. The papers told you it was forbidden. Of course you couldn't save him."

"'Forbidden' isn't the same as 'impossible,'" Delphine said in a churlish tone, but she knew he was right. She fell silent. Alexander didn't deserve to have her snap at him.

Ysabeau slowed to walk alongside her. "There's no shame in being afraid, Delphine." Her voice was low and smooth, washing over Delphine's bruised heart and taking some of the pain away. "The trick is to recognize the fear, accept it, and decide you won't allow it to control you. When fear controls you, it turns to hatred. Don't let that happen to you."

Delphine sniffed and wiped her nose on her cloak. "Easy for you to say," she muttered. "You don't have the fate of the kingdom resting on your shoulders."

"No, that's true." Ysabeau smiled wryly. "I only have the fate of the *savior* of the kingdom on my shoulders. As do Alexander, and Cornichonne, and Bearnois. We're all here for you."

"You do know that, yes?" chimed in Alexander.

Delphine was unable to find the right words.

Buzzing loudly, Bearnois floated from his perch above Cornichonne toward Delphine. She put out a paw to stroke his fur. "I know I'm not on my own." She focused on looking at Bearnois so she wouldn't start crying. "Thank you."

Alexander spoke slowly. "I am here for you, my lady. Always."

Delphine gulped. Every day she was becoming more attached to Alexander, and more afraid of losing him . . . which she very well might if she kept exploring the forbidden magic. Delphine shook her head, trying to focus on what she could control.

"I have to find out more about Midnight," she announced. She remembered Flore had said the city to the east was swarming with rats. "I need to find Midnight's minions before they find me. It'll be the last thing they'll expect. If I'm careful, I'll be able to observe them unnoticed, get information. Their weaknesses. Maybe even Midnight's location." *A lair atop a mountain,* she remembered Blé saying.

"So we're going to Montrenasse-sur-Terre?" For the first time, Ysabeau's voice wavered.

Delphine nodded, trying to appear brave. "We'll see what we can learn there."

Alexander brightened. "Montrenasse is reputed to have the finest mouse armor workshop in the kingdom. Perhaps we could outfit ourselves while we're in town. I once dueled a noblemouse wearing Montrenasse armor, and every slice of my sword slid off his breastplate like butter from a hot knife."

"Then you must have lost?" Delphine said, relieved to be slipping back into their familiar banter. She glanced at Ysabeau, and the pawmaid stifled a small laugh.

"Certainly not!" Alexander puffed out his chest. "I . . . ah . . . tricked him into thinking that the ringing of the bell tower meant the guards were about to attack, and he turned tail and fled. Straight into a rainstorm, I might add." He paused thoughtfully. "Montrenasse-sur-Terre is *also* rumored to have excellent cheeses!"

If only I could snatch a moment in Montrenasse to search for the tapestry workshop and clues about the Threaded, Delphine thought, but she didn't let herself say it out loud.

She had to stay focused on the immediate threat: Midnight.

CHAPTER 8

It was overcast when the group struck out in the direction of Montrenasse-sur-Terre. Every so often, Ysabeau glanced around and confirmed they were still going east.

"How can you tell?" asked Delphine. "The sun is hidden."

Ysabeau pointed at the trunk of the closest tree. "What do you see?"

Alexander squinted. "There's a hole in the trunk shaped exactly like a cream puff."

Ysabeau groaned, but Delphine caught her smiling. "Look at the moss."

Delphine's eyes widened. "It's only growing on the north side of the trunk!"

"That's right. This greenish-gray moss, we call it North Wind's Breath."

Delphine examined the moss, committing it to memory. Then she turned back to Ysabeau. "Did you ever regret leaving all this for the castle?"

Ysabeau began walking again and Delphine trotted alongside her. "No, I wanted to explore and see more of the kingdom. The castle was one of the first places I visited, and I realized that being Princess Petits-Oiseaux's pawmaid would give me the chance to travel more than I ever could on my own."

"That's so clever." Ysabeau suddenly seemed very worldly to Delphine, who had never traveled beyond her local towns before she had been thrown into this quest.

Ysabeau gave Delphine's paw a friendly squeeze. "You've had so many adventures already! Meeting a ghost, nearly getting eaten by a fish—"

"It was a *pike!*" declared Alexander from behind them. "Not just any fish! An enormous, vicious pike!"

Ysabeau traded a glance with Delphine and they both giggled. "Delphine, I'm so glad we met. I had a good feeling about you from the minute you stepped into the princess's chambers."

"I'm glad, too." Delphine squeezed her paw in return. Ysabeau brought something special to the group: a sense of ease and calm. It was hard to feel too worried when she was around. Inspired by Ysabeau's faith in her, Delphine drew out her needle and began some target practice as they traveled. She created a bloom of silver sparks around every outcropping of North Wind's Breath that she could spot on the tree trunks and felt a little more powerful with each one. The magic wasn't becoming easier, but it *was* becoming more familiar. *Almost like learning a musical instrument*, she thought. Noticing Ysabeau watching her, Delphine drew a little patch of snow-white flowers out of the ground in front of her new friend.

Ysabeau clapped her paws. "It's like the magic is becoming part of you, Delphine."

It's true, thought Delphine. That was exactly what it was like. The magic was becoming interwoven into her body and mind.

They camped that night inside the crumbling remains of a human strongbox. The rusty padlock had been rendered pointless by years of termites and rot eating away at the wood panels.

"How did it get out here in the middle of the forest?" wondered Delphine as they clambered inside through a hole large enough for even Cornichonne.

"Some human must have carried it out here," murmured Ysabeau.

The strongbox was half full of gold coins marked with the crest of the royal humans. Each coin was large enough to be a bed for a mouse . . . albeit a painfully cold, hard bed. Nothing at all edible could be found. "It's too bad the human didn't bother to put some provisions into their strongbox while they were at it," Alexander mumbled as they tried to get comfortable.

Cornichonne began to sing. It was an old ditty Delphine recognized, the story of three mouse sisters who outwitted a clan of rat bandits for a chest of gold.

Why would someone leave all this gold in the middle of nowhere? thought Delphine as she drifted off to sleep.

She dreamt she was back home, in front of Château Desjardins. She stepped through the open door and wandered through the familiar hallways, following a fine silver thread that led away into the darkness. She walked and walked, but no matter how many corners she turned or stairs she climbed, the thread stretched onward. . . .

She awoke exhausted the next morning.

Before they left the strongbox behind, she chipped a few flakes off the edge of one coin. It would be enough to stock up on provisions in Montrenasse-sur-Terre. Delphine carefully stowed the gold flakes in her pocket.

"Are you sure they won't fall out?" asked Alexander.

Delphine thought for a moment, then pulled out her needle and ran the point along the pocket's edge. The fabric twisted back on itself, pulling the pocket closed. She winked. "I'm sure."

The next night, as Delphine chopped up a wizened root into the meager soup bubbling over the fire, she found herself watching Alexander. He was hard at work removing dead thistles that had gotten stuck in Cornichonne's fur. Her thoughts strayed as they often did, back to the Winterberry Ball at the château, how he had gazed into her eyes as they had danced. She snuck another glance at him across the twigfire. There was something so kind and handsome about his face when he wasn't putting on airs. And those aristocratic ears—

His head popped up as if he could tell that she had been watching him. She felt her own ears burn. "Dinnertime!" she called to him, hoping it would explain her gaze. She poured the soup into acorn bowls, and they all drank heartily.

Alexander smacked his lips, even though the soup was thin and tasteless. "Delicious! Makes me think of the time I was the guest of honor at a fourteen-course meal. It was hosted by a vole who only ate vegetables that were purple, so imagine . . ."

"You don't say." Delphine chuckled. She let herself savor her soup a little more slowly while Alexander wove his tale.

After another day or two of travel, the forest gave way to pastures and fields, dotted with copses of young trees. At first even Bearnois seemed relaxed, buzzing happily to and fro in the winter sun. But slowly, signs of the rats' destruction began to appear. Claw marks on abandoned mouse farmers' carts, a squirrel home with the door torn off, the remains of a mouse cottage still smoldering from the fire that had burned it to the ground. Bearnois grew edgier with each passing day, burning out his reserves of energy from buzzing so frantically that finally he had to be coaxed to perch on Cornichonne's back and rest as they traveled.

Then came the gutted remains of an entire mouse village that had existed inside the walls of a human barn. It lay in waste, destroyed by the rats as they'd ravaged their way across the countryside. *Looking for* me, thought Delphine with a pit in her stomach. The village had been destroyed because of her, the same as how the rats had pillaged mouse cities during the War to End All Wars. History was repeating itself.

The closer they got to Montrenasse-sur-Terre, the worse it became. They passed stragglers fleeing for their lives. They came across little piles of belongings, clearly abandoned on the side of the road when they had become too heavy or cumbersome for the fleeing mice to carry.

Once, they came upon a mouse's wedding ring lying in the dirt, a single link of a human necklace chain that had been formed into a solid circle. "Nobody would have left that behind on purpose," said Ysabeau solemnly. They left it where it lay, all silently hoping its owner might return for it someday.

Delphine kept practicing with the needle. But fear was growing inside her. She had figured out how to gather snowflakes into dazzling flurries, how to crack a stone in two, how to summon tree roots up out of the ground and twist them around tails and paws. These things might stop the rats who worked for Midnight. But she knew they wouldn't be enough against Midnight himself.

Over and over, she examined the strange runes on the needle's shaft, hoping to unlock their meaning and tap into stronger magic. By now, she knew their shapes by heart. But she still had no idea what they signified.

The strain of holding herself together in front of her friends stretched her nerves as tight as the strings of a violin. One night as they all huddled around their little campfire, she couldn't take it anymore. "I'll be back soon," she announced to no one in particular, and headed across the abandoned field toward a copse of trees. On her own, beneath the sweeping branches, she finally let herself cry.

The rats' carnage had only been made more evident the last few days, and she had no idea what to do. She wasn't only going to fail her friends. She was going to fail an entire kingdom.

Hopeless anger and hatred washed over her. She threw the needle down onto the ground. As it flew from her grasp, blue light arced from her paws.

Was that . . . ? It looked like the blue lightning in her nightmares. A terrible hope flared. She snatched the needle, and it crackled back to life. A sharp shot of lightning erupted, slamming into a tree trunk. She gulped, then narrowed her eyes and let herself dip down farther into the fury that roiled inside her. Another cold blue bolt burned itself into a tree.

"Ha!" She let her hatred for the rats take control. It streamed out of the needle in jagged lines, bright enough to hurt her eyes.

A twig cracked behind her. She spun to point the needle at whoever had been spying on her.

Alexander. Not spying at all, merely coming into the copse from the direction of camp.

"Would you care for some dinner?" He glanced quickly at the blue burns still smoking on the tree trunks.

"Ah . . . yes. Thank you." She lowered her needle. She waited to hear him ask about the marks on the trees, but he merely turned back toward camp.

She followed him across the frozen field in silence. It wasn't until they had nearly reached the camp that he paused. "Delfie." He cleared his throat a few times, then finally said, "You know I believe in you."

"I do." It came out more stiffly than she had intended. "And I appreciate it."

"I believe in the good in you," Alexander said, speaking more deliberately this time. Then he hurried into camp.

The next day they traveled quietly. The sky above them was as flat and gray as the road they walked along. Delphine wanted desperately to talk to Alexander, but she couldn't figure out how to begin. They camped on the ridge of a hill. After dinner, as Alexander sat close to the fire warming his paws, Delphine slowly approached him.

"Alexander?" Her stomach was doing flip-flops. "Are you—" She gulped. "Are you angry with me? I thought—after what you saw yesterday—"

"Oh Delfie." He reached out and pulled her down to sit beside him. "I could never be angry at you."

She felt the knot in her stomach untie itself. Before she lost her nerve, she leaned in toward him until her head was resting on his shoulder, her face buried against his neck.

His fur was soft and warm. He spoke very quietly. "I'm afraid for you."

There was nothing more to say.

They awoke to the sight of distant smoke in the early-morning light, rising slowly from the next hill in thin streams. And on the hill beyond loomed the high walls of a human city: Montrenasse-sur-Terre.

"Looks like all we have to do is follow the fires," said Alexander under his breath. They began the trek across the valley, through the remains of mouse villages and toward the foreboding sight.

※　※　※

Montrenasse-sur-Terre's thick city walls rose up before them, somber and unyielding, built by humans centuries earlier. But Delphine hadn't come this far to be stopped by a wall. She tipped her head back and surveyed the impenetrable surface. Could they climb up the stone? What about Cornichonne?

She was interrupted by a faint whuffle a few feet away. They all turned to see the cat peering through a little grate near the bottom of the wall—from the inside.

"How—" Delphine had to laugh. Leave it to Cornichonne

to figure out how to get through before the mice did. The cat came back out through the crack she had discovered. It was barely large enough for Cornichonne to squeeze through, but the mice passed with ease. Bearnois buzzed along nervously behind them, lagging until Ysabeau pulled out a dried flower to coax him forward.

As soon as they were inside the walls they could hear sounds of rat skirmishes coming from corners beneath human buildings and down human side streets. A faint mouse squeal trailed on the morning air like a thread of smoke. Ysabeau shivered.

Alexander squared his shoulders and placed one paw on the pommel of his sword. "So where do we start?"

Delphine pointed ahead to an empty narrow alleyway. "Let's see if we can find any mice who are still living here. If the rats have been loose-lipped about the location of Midnight's lair— or why exactly he wants the needle so badly—maybe the mice have overheard." She tiptoed toward the entrance of the alley, keeping to the shadows, and the rest followed.

Alexander tugged on her sleeve. "I'm sure he wants the needle for nefarious purposes," he whispered.

"I hadn't thought of that," replied Delphine, deadpan. Ysabeau gave a tiny smile.

Alexander sniffed and pulled the hood of his cloak down so low that his whiskers pointed out elegantly on either side like river reeds. If the overall scene hadn't been so tense, Delphine would have laughed out loud.

The human buildings lining the narrow alley loomed high on either side of them. It was like walking through a long, dim cave. Ivy grew haphazardly across the walls, digging its tendrils into the mortar that was slowly crumbling between the stones.

Bearnois gave a sudden frantic hum. "Wait," Ysabeau murmured. Delphine knew what that meant: danger ahead.

The bee froze, his buzzing growing wild. Cornichonne's ears lay flat against her head.

"*Mangy curs!*" A filthy, yellow-fanged rat flew from a second-story human window, plummeting downward. He twisted in the air, trying to land on his paws, but he wasn't fast enough. He hit the cobblestones tail-first with a horrid cracking sound and shrieked.

Chittering laughter came from the window. Three other rats peered down at the fallen rat, evil grins on their faces. "Serves you right, Pinoird!" shouted one. Her raspy voice made Delphine's fur stand on end.

Pinoird groaned. "You pushed me! You—" But he never had a chance to finish what he was about to say. The rats in the window had spotted Delphine and her companions. In the blink of an eye, they scurried down the ivy growing in the wall to the street below.

"Fresh meat," said the leader rat, and the other two snickered. "These little mice don't look near frightened enough yet, do they? I say we show 'em why they should be afraid."

All three leapt at the mice, fangs bared. One swung a

wooden club at Alexander and he parried her attack desperately. Delphine ran to join him, sparks already flaming from her needle.

Cornichonne threw herself at another rat, swiping with her paws. The force sent him flying across the alley. He smashed into the wall and fell to the ground, moaning.

The third rat was headed straight toward Ysabeau. Delphine watched in horror as he slashed his filthy claws deep across the pawmaid's chest. She crumpled to the ground. The rat closed in, but Bearnois was upon him, a blur of wings. The rat screamed a terrible high scream and fell. A bee stinger protruded from his shoulder where Bearnois had stung him. In another twitch, the rat lay dead.

"Ysabeau!" Delphine threw herself at her friend, who was sprawled out on the cobblestones. Ysabeau coughed, her mouth wet and dark. Her eyes were already glazing over.

A cry tore out of Delphine. If only she could turn back time and push Ysabeau out of the rat's way.

The needle tingled hot in her paws. She looked down, a wild thought bubbling, so wild that she couldn't think of anything else. She leapt up and swung her needle in a counterclockwise circle through the air, picturing a clock face and trying to push the hands backward. The papers had said not to meddle with the passage of time . . . which meant it *had* to be possible. Didn't it? She had to try.

Nothing happened. She redoubled her efforts, blocking out the sounds of Ysabeau's desperate coughs. If she could only rewind the clock by a few seconds . . . She gritted her teeth, feeling blood dripping from her nose from the effort. Her whole body was shaking. Still nothing happened.

"Delphine!" Alexander's arms were around her, pulling her backward, ripping the needle from her paw. "What are you doing? You're bleeding!"

She stumbled and fell next to Ysabeau. The sight of her friend's wounds brought her back to reality.

"Ysabeau, stay with me!"

Ysabeau clutched her paws to her chest as if trying to hold herself together. But she didn't look back at Delphine. She was staring past her, tears running down her cheeks.

Delphine realized what Ysabeau was seeing. Bearnois lay on the ground, the beat of his wings slowing. His antennae were wilted and limp. Royal bumblebees could sting only once. He had given his life to save Ysabeau.

"No!" gasped Ysabeau, but her voice was thick and she began to cough again. Alexander knelt by her, wrapping his cloak around her as tightly as he could. He scooped her up into his arms.

"Alexander!" Delphine could hear herself screaming, even as she reached down to pick up Bearnois. "We have to get them to safety!"

The other two rats had pulled themselves up from the

cobblestones. She could feel the needle burning cold against her paw where she still clutched it, her arms wrapped awkwardly around Bearnois's limp body. She gave a last glance at the rats. If only she had been able to corner one of them, get some information out of him. A location for Midnight, a direction, *something*. But this was so much more important now. If Ysabeau died because Delphine had insisted they come to this city . . .

She didn't dare think about Bearnois.

The rats were closing in. She spotted a tiny hole in a nearby wall, little more than a crack. She prayed it wasn't a dead end. There was nowhere else to go.

She raced as fast as she could toward the hole, Alexander following behind. "Run!" Delphine yelled back to Cornichonne. "We'll meet you at the front gates of the city!" She saw doubt in her friend's eyes. "I promise!" she cried.

Cornichonne lowered to her haunches, ready to leap at the rats but watching the mice head toward safety. She was waiting to make sure they made it into the hole. "Cornichonne! Don't risk it! If you get hurt, too . . ." Delphine was out of breath. She prayed that Cornichonne would listen to her and head back toward the safety of the busier streets.

It was a tight squeeze but the four of them made it through the crack in the stone wall. Then she heard Cornichonne yowling as she ran back down the alley, letting Delphine know that she was heading toward the city gates. The cat's voice trailed into the distance.

Ysabeau was panting in rapid, shallow breaths. The sound sent shivers down Delphine's spine.

Ahead, the crack continued downward, turning into a narrow tunnel through the wall. She followed it, cradling Bearnois, Alexander behind her with Ysabeau still in his arms. The passage led through the cellar of the building and into another wall. They kept going. Tunnels joined and branched off again. They were scurrying from cellar to cellar, beneath the buildings of the human city. Where would it be safe to reemerge? And how would they find any help once they did? But they had to try. As soon as they came to a passage heading back up toward the surface, they followed it as quickly as they could.

It dumped them out on a quiet side street, lined with human handworkers' shopfronts. Furriers, farriers, cobbler shops, and more. Most had corresponding mouse businesses in the foundations of the buildings. Delphine felt a desperate spark of hope. Now they had to find one that was open.

Then she spotted a human shop with a richly ornamented tapestry hanging in the window, heavy with detailing in golden threads. Could that be . . . ? The coincidence was too big to ignore. She nodded toward the building and Alexander's eyes widened. At the bottom of the wall stood a mouse door, and a window displaying a mouse-size tapestry.

"Is that a tapestry workshop?" He was breathing hard as he clutched Ysabeau's limp body.

"Maybe we were supposed to end up there after all."

Still carrying Ysabeau and Bearnois, they scurried across the street between passing carts and horses, watching for more rats. Delphine raised her paw to knock, and the little round mouse door fell open beneath her touch.

VALENTINE OOZED BETWEEN THE THRONE room doors. There wasn't much moonlight tonight, and that was the way the ermine liked it. Darkness was her friend. She picked her way across the floor, curling back her lip in disgust when one of her paws sank into something squelchy and cold. She had no desire to find out what that was. Fastidious as always, she paused to wipe her paw on the black velvet cloak draped across the throne, then continued toward her goal.

Above the long-dead fireplace, above the mouse skulls lined up on the mantelpiece, hung eleven huge silver needles. She gazed up at them. Midnight acted as if these needles were more valuable than gold. How many times had he gabbled about how he would take over the world with them? All he needed was the twelfth, he kept repeating.

She curled her lip again, remembering their conversation in the library. His voice still rang in her ears. She was tired of his theatrics, tired of his overblown bombast and posturing. Calling himself *king*. She snickered. Maybe now that she was leaving this place behind, she would start calling herself King Valentine. Why not? It had a nice ring to it.

After Midnight had stormed out of the old library, Valentine decided it was high time to strike out on her own. Perhaps it hadn't been a coincidence that she'd been reading Mousechiavelli's *The Prince*—that knowledge would serve her well on the road. After packing her belongings, she began nosing around the fortress in search of little treasures she could sell for easy gold. Then she thought of the needles. If Midnight treasured them that much, surely others would as well.

Now in the throne room, she dropped her travel bag on the floor and slithered up onto the mantelpiece. She had the first needle in her paw when the doors slammed open.

"Valentine." The voice was low and dangerous. "I should have known you'd try something like this." Even in the dark, Valentine could recognize Mezzo by her blaze. The white stripe of fur down the center of her face gleamed in the moonlight.

Valentine slipped to the ground and grinned at the rat guard, her fangs gleaming. Mezzo looked entirely unfazed. Perhaps Valentine had underestimated her after all.

"Those belong to Midnight," Mezzo hissed. Her mouth was set in a hard line.

"Midnight is a fool!" snarled Valentine. "He's using you, and you're a fool as well for letting yourself be used."

Something dark flickered in Mezzo's eyes, and Valentine found herself taking a step back. "I know you're planning to leave," said the rat. "I won't stop you. But I swear by my sister's life that if you do anything to endanger my good standing with Midnight, I will hunt you down myself."

Valentine smiled a broad, disingenuous smile. "As you wish." She snatched up her travel bag and waltzed out through the doors quickly, before Mezzo could change her mind.

As soon as she was out of sight of the throne room, she heaved a sigh of irritation. She hadn't needed the needles. She had merely liked imagining the rage on Midnight's face when he discovered they were gone.

She spotted a human pocketwatch being used as a clock in a nearby alcove. Gold body, precious gems inlaid in the numbers . . . she could sell that for a pawful of coins. She shoved it into her travel bag and headed on down the hall, keeping her eyes peeled.

By the time Valentine let herself out through the main doors, the bag was heavy on her shoulder. She set off across the empty expanse of stones, whistling to herself. Her snow-white fur glimmered in the moonlight. She would figure out where she was headed when she got there.

the Brocciu moon

Chapter 9

Delphine stumbled into the tapestry workshop, too afraid for her friends to worry about the bloody pawmarks she was leaving on the door. Bearnois was barely breathing. Delphine cast about in desperation, her eyes so filled with tears that the room blurred before her.

A matronly mouse with round white cheeks appeared. Another mouse lifted Bearnois from Delphine's arms. She heard the door being wiped clean and shut behind them. A cool paw wiped the tears from her cheeks.

"My poor child," soothed the round-cheeked weaver mouse. "Was it the rats?"

Delphine could do nothing but nod. She stared at Bearnois, now cradled by the younger mouse. Both weaver mice were garbed head to toe in fine linen, rich with embroidery. A third mouse appeared as if summoned, reaching out for Ysabeau. Alexander surrendered her limp form, still wrapped in his velvet cloak. One corner of the cloak dragged on the rug of the room, leaving behind a trail of dirt and muck.

The motherly mouse regarded Delphine, her pale eyes filled with concern. "Which band of rats was it this time? Was it Lymon's crew again?"

"I don't know." Delphine took a shuddering gasp, her gaze fixed on Ysabeau lying so deathly still in the young mouse's arms. "Can you help my friends? Please?" She suddenly remembered the gold shavings in her pocket and fumbled to dig them out. "We can pay. We have gold."

But the mouse had already turned and gestured at the other two. "What are you waiting for? Take them to the infirmary!" She turned back to Delphine and nipped up the gold shavings from her paw. "Of course we will help. So many of our own weavers have been injured by the rats. It's getting harder to live here every day, but I refuse to go. This workshop has been here for over a century, and it is my home." She paused, tilting her head. "What part of the city are you from? Did you not know to avoid Lymon's band of bruisers?"

Delphine raised a paw to push back her hood. She discovered she was still clutching her needle.

At the sight, the weaver's breath caught in her throat. Her eyes blinked rapidly. But in another instant, the expression of surprise was neatly wiped away. Her gaze slid back to Delphine's face, as if she were making a point of not watching Delphine resheathe the needle.

"We've traveled here from . . ." Delphine paused. From Château Trois-Arbres? From the castle? From somewhere in between? ". . . from the other side of the kingdom," she fumbled. She wasn't sure why she didn't want to be more specific.

The weaver gave Delphine a good look up and down. "You poor thing!" Sweeping Delphine into a warm hug, she tutted. "Those heathen rats! Their king keeps sending more and more of them south every day, he does."

At the feel of the weaver's arms around her, so like her mother's embrace, Delphine wanted more than ever to break down. "So you'll help our friends?"

"Naturally, my dear!" The weaver gave her a sympathetic smile. "Come in, come in. I am Julite. Welcome to our workshop."

She led Delphine and Alexander along a warm, dark hallway.

Julite's nails clicked on the stone floor, but the walls were oddly soft when Delphine stumbled in exhaustion and fell against one. Julite saw her expression and chuckled.

"Skeins of wool, arranged on the bottommost shelves of the humans' tapestry workshop. We're right on the other side. It makes a lovely wall, doesn't it? And it's peachy for keeping the heat in during these freezing winters."

Delphine had to agree. The whole warren of workshop hallways and workrooms was surprisingly cozy, given how brutally cold it had been outside. And there was a familiar scent in the air, of clover and sheep. Of course—it was the wool. She remembered that smell from her childhood, when she would play hide-and-seek in Cinderella's knitting basket, burrowing among the skeins of yarn.

Julite left them in a little antechamber, surrounded on all three sides by walls of human yarn skeins. "Sit," she ordered in her no-nonsense way. "I'm going to summon a healer for your friends, but you need to rest as well."

There was nothing Delphine wanted to hear less. She tried to head back into the hall but Julite blocked her, kindly but firmly. "You can't do anything for your friends right now. You've already done the best thing you could by bringing them here. Now get some rest." She closed the door behind her, and they could hear the quiet clicks of her toenails on the stone floor, fading away.

Delphine paced, her tail twitching from side to side. Then she noticed Alexander. He had lain down on a loose skein of yarn, his eyes already half-closed. "Alexander, really!"

He startled and opened his eyes wide. "I wasn't sleeping!"

"Of course you weren't." But she sank down next to him, already feeling sorry for having woken him. Now that the terror of their flight through the underground tunnels had passed, a bone-deep exhaustion was washing over her. She let herself lean back on the soft, warm yarn. It squished up around her in a cozy embrace.

Alexander reached out and took her paw. They lay side by side, eyes shut, feeling the warmth of each other's paws.

"We'll rest for a moment," she said, her words already slurring. "Only a moment. Then we'll go check . . . on Ysabeau and Bearnois. . . ."

✳ ✳ ✳

Delphine dreamt she was wandering through endless hallways deep underground, still following the silver thread. *"Did you read the tapestries of Château Trois Arbres?"* came a voice, but there was nobody there. Shafts of moonlight made names gleam on the walls. She tried to remember the names, certain they would be important, but the thread was growing tarnished in her paws. It pulled her onward, and the names were left behind.

She was startled awake when she rolled over and slid off the skein, landing hard on the stone floor. Her yelp awoke Alexander. He sat up, rubbing his eyes.

Delphine looked around, but there were no windows to see the position of the sun in the sky. "How long did we sleep?"

Alexander shrugged. "Probably not long. I must say . . . a ball of yarn makes a better bed even than the thistledown puffs at the castle. I shall have to recommend it to the princess when I return." He straightened his waistcoat.

They ventured into the corridors in search of Ysabeau and Bearnois. It didn't take them long to find the workshop's make-shift infirmary. It took them even less time to learn from the mouse stationed at the door that an apprentice weaver had been sent to summon the healer, and under no circumstances was anyone permitted to enter the infirmary.

Delphine was itching to shove past the self-important guard mouse, but Alexander gently touched her arm. He had gotten good at knowing what she was thinking.

"Did the apprentice leave recently?" he asked the guard mouse, his voice smooth and pleasant.

The mouse nodded. "Mother Julite sent her off not long ago."

"Well, there you have it." Alexander turned to Delphine. "All we have to do is be patient and wait. I've seen our healers at work at the castle, many times. They always know what to do. We need to trust." He sounded downright calm.

Delphine frowned. Didn't he understand the severity of the

situation? She opened her mouth again, and he squeezed her paw hard.

"Delfie!" he said, with a smile plastered on his face. "The tapestries!" She glanced at him, wary of this bizarrely upbeat Alexander. "This is *the* tapestry workshop, right? Let's go see if we can find any good ones!" He looked again at the guard, and his voice grew even more calm and friendly. "Where might we find the *older* tapestries?"

The guard mouse pointed at a broad oak door. "Through there, down the stone stairs. The archive is at the end of the hall on your left. But it's been under renovation for a while. Not sure if they ever finished."

"Thank you kindly!" Alexander took Delphine's elbow and headed for the dark oak door, keeping up his chipper attitude until the door had swung shut behind them. Once they pawed their way down the stone staircase, his ears drooped. "It's so hard to act like everything is fine when you're frightened half to death."

Delphine gave a sigh of relief. "I thought you had lost it up there."

"You catch more bees with honey; I knew they'd be more willing to help if we were pleasant." He shook his head. "But I'm frightened for Ysabeau and Bearnois, too. They don't . . . I mean . . ." He cleared his throat. "Look, we've done all we can. We might as well go look at some tapestries while we wait. Agreed?"

Delphine caught the concern for her in his eyes. On impulse, she took his paw in hers. His ears went a little pink. Delphine found herself blushing. But he didn't feel *that way* about her. Did he?

Paws still clasped, they reached the door to the archive. There was a tattered scrap of paper stuck onto a nail in the door. In small, neatly written letters it said CLOSED FOR RENOVATION. But the thick layer of dust on the door handle suggested that nobody had come by for quite some time.

Delphine's shoulders slumped. "It's *closed?*" After she had come all this way, and endangered the lives of two of her friends in the process. "Beetles and boils," she mumbled. "I wish I'd never even suggested we come to this stupid city."

"Poppycock," replied Alexander. "First, this isn't why you suggested coming to Montrenasse. Second, it was fate that we ended up here at the workshop, so we're going to find out why." He grabbed the metal latch and shoved against the door until it slowly creaked open. The grating protest of the rusted hinges echoed in the empty hall. Delphine smiled. Good old Alexander.

They found themselves in a huge, high-ceilinged stone hall that stretched before them. The air had the cold, musty odor of a space that had been closed up for many years. Ladders leaned against walls and stacks of dusty stones lay on the floor, still waiting for renovations to recommence.

Delphine gasped at the sight of so many old tapestries hanging along both walls. They were larger than any she had ever seen, even larger than those hanging in the hall of tapestries at Château Trois Arbres.

"Philomène was right," she breathed.

She tiptoed along the hall, taking in the scenes of the Threaded. There were so many! Mice collecting morning dew from flowers and transforming it into diamonds, with real jewels woven right into the tapestry. And nonmagical activities, too: training hawkworms as hunting pets, saddling up their snail mounts, painting and singing and dancing. Had her ancestor done all these things? With, perhaps, some of the very Threaded shown here in these tapestries? Was her ancestor herself in any of them? Delphine searched the backgrounds for a baby cradled in the arms of any of the mice, but there were none.

One tapestry featured two mice she recognized instantly: Arachne and Rhapso. As usual, a spindle hung from Arachne's paws by a silver thread. But unlike any image Delphine had seen before of the two legendary mice, there was someone—or something—standing between them. A suit of gleaming silver armor, visor lowered as if ready for battle. She racked her mind but could remember no mention of silver armor in the tales of Arachne and Rhapso that she knew.

The next tapestry made Delphine forget all about the strange silver armor. It was a sweeping scene of a castle floating in the clouds. Tiny mice were busy all throughout the castle and the clouds, some holding the needles of the Threaded, others dressed as regular folk.

Delphine thought about the mosaic she had seen in the hidden room of the Dead City, how it bore a stunning resemblance to the castle depicted here. Yet again, Madame Philomène's voice echoed in her mind. *"Once upon a time, the Threaded lived in a castle in the clouds."* Who knew what answers might lie within those walls?

And for a moment, Delphine allowed her thoughts to float up to the legendary castle, away from her worries and woes.

CHAPTER 10

Delphine examined tapestry after tapestry, still trying to distract herself from her nagging fears for Ysabeau and Bearnois. The ancient weavings held more scenes of the Threaded than Delphine had ever imagined could exist. They frolicked, spun magic, climbed snow-covered trees, and stood triumphant on islands in the ocean. But nowhere did Delphine find anything that could be considered a clue to the location of their castle.

"I guess I had been expecting more," she said to Alexander, her whiskers drooping. "A list of places, maybe. Or a map."

"At least we've learned how much they love moonlight." Alexander pointed to an illustrated scene of several Threaded standing atop a tower beneath a full moon. The moonlight streamed down in thin threads and seemed to wrap around the paws of one mouse. Another mouse was winding a silvery strand into a ball. Delphine peered closer but couldn't make heads or tails of what it was supposed to depict.

She started opening the doors lining the back wall of the archive, desperate to find even a scrap of useful information. She couldn't bear to leave empty-pawed. Most of the doors revealed storage closets full of cleaning and preservation materials for the ancient tapestries. Some led to stairways. The last one opened onto a dark, crumbling stone room with a massive pile of rubble nearly covering the back wall.

"Nothing in there but a caved-in ceiling," Alexander said, moving to close the door.

But Delphine stopped him. "Wait." She inched closer, pulling out the needle and letting it glow gently in her paw. The soft light illuminated the room, and she could see that the ceiling was still intact.

"The ceiling didn't cave in," she replied. Her gaze traveled up the pile of rubble. There at the top, lit by the light of the needle, peeked the edge of an old stone archway.

Alexander joined her. "Then where did all those stones come from?"

"That's what I'm wondering. Unless . . ." She peered at the bit of exposed archway above the rubble. "Could someone have put those stones here on purpose, to hide something?"

She flicked her needle sideways. With a silvery whoosh, the topmost stones flew from the pile, crashing into the walls.

Alexander yelped and leapt backward. "A little warning, please!"

Bit by bit, she used the needle's magic to shove the rest of the stones out of the way.

A pitch-black doorway stood before them.

She and Alexander stepped into a dark passage. Taking a deep breath, Delphine tiptoed forward.

At the far end, through a hand-carved wooden door, they emerged into a tiny suite of windowless rooms. The walls were awash in the glow of Delphine's needle. She thought back to the room of the Threaded in the Dead City, but that had been lavish, high-ceilinged, filled with morning light. These rooms were tiny, with no windows. Still, there was something so similar about the two, as if they had both been designed as safe spaces for times of danger.

"What a funny layout," said Alexander, peering around. The room was not quite square, with tiny triangular closets off to either side. A doorway ahead led through a sort of sitting area and into a bedroom that looked like it had curved walls.

Delphine's eyes sparkled. "These rooms were built right into the walls of the human building, to make use of hidden spaces. We have rooms like this back home all over Château Desjardins, all in funny shapes."

"But why hide these rooms from the other mice?"

Delphine shook her head. That was one question she couldn't answer.

In the main room stood a mouse table and chairs. A neat rag rug was spread on the stone floor. Next to a large sideboard was a stove, already filled with twigs. Shelves of stoneware dishes, ancient onionskin books, and seedpods lined the room.

Delphine peeked into the triangular rooms. Both were stacked full with kindling, bags of grain, jars of dried fruits and salted nuts, and every other foodstuff a mouse might need to survive for years in hiding. Rows and rows of hand-poured candles stood at attention.

"Someone stored these items here with plans to return," whispered Alexander. They passed through the sitting area into the bedroom, where a beautiful tapestry hung from one wall above a four-poster bed. Dried yew branches formed the four posts, extending upward to graze the low stone ceiling. A walnut-shell crib sat at the end of the bed.

Neatly folded clothing lay in the drawers of a dresser, with a shard of looking glass and a bone-dry ewer and basin on top. "But why? And when? This room . . . These things are *ancient.*"

She noticed a pair of ladies' shoes placed carefully on the rug next to the bed, and a pair of gentlemice's shoes on the other side. "Those shoes haven't been in style for a hundred years. Nor have any of those clothes." It was clearly a place of refuge for mice of long ago, but it was so clean and tidy, it seemed as if it had never been used.

"Those ladies' shoes," Alexander pointed out. "Maybe they belonged to your mystery mouse on the run?"

"She was never here," responded Delphine. "At least, not that we know of. I suppose anything's possible, but it seems so unlikely. Château Trois Arbres, the music school, the monastery . . . all those lie in the central and southern areas of the kingdom. Could she really have made it up here to the north as well?"

She gazed around as she spoke, thinking out loud. "Also, this isn't a room for someone on the run. This is a room where someone could hide from danger for years. They had a lot of food stored." She pointed out a small opening cut into the stone wall and placed her paw inside. "There's fresh water dripping through here, probably from the rooftop. Melting snow in the winter, rain in the summer."

"Clever," Alexander admitted. "I don't know if I would have figured that out."

"Well, well," Delphine teased him. "The marvelous Alexander, admitting somebody else is smarter than he is?"

"Perish the thought!"

Delphine stared at small holes set into the walls, each with a pipe end sticking out. She remembered seeing something similar at the castle when she had visited Princess Petits-Oiseaux. "What in the world are these?"

Alexander came up to investigate. "Ah! Whisper-holes! Useful for those who wish to overhear the conversations of others. Or in this case . . . perhaps so the residents of these rooms could keep an ear on what was happening outside?"

Delphine nodded, thinking. "They could hear when it was finally safe to come out. But we still don't know why they thought they would need to hide in the first place."

"Maybe there are more clues here than we realize," he murmured. He ran his paws along the edge of a delicate writing table. There was a soft springing sound, and a panel popped open. "Aha!"

Delphine blinked. "How did you know that would be there?"

"I recognize the style of writing desk." He reached inside the dark space and pulled out a bundle of thick envelopes and papers, tied together with a length of cobalt-blue embroidery floss.

They both sat down at the little kitchen table. Alexander handed the bundle to Delphine. The old onionskin paper crumbled against her touch as she unwrapped the embroidery floss.

The letters had been folded and refolded many times, clearly read over and over. The dates were all out of order. Most were from someone named Elodie, addressed to another mouse by the name of Maturin. A few were Maturin's responses.

Delphine's breath caught in her throat. "Elodie! Wasn't that one of the names of the Threaded on the tapestry at Château Trois Arbres?" She strained to remember.

"Are you sure?"

"I . . ." She shook her head. "I don't know." She skipped down the page, her head bent low to decipher the faded copperplate.

". . . but until then, I hold you in my thoughts. I am simply so glad you could visit me at the castle for as long as you did. I often reflect on how wonderful it was that we even met. To think I nearly pretended to be ill so I could avoid a tedious trip to a tapestry workshop. I should never have forgiven myself, but how could I have known? My darling Maturin, you live in my heart and mind.

"Tail and whiskers, I am yours—Elodie

"P.S. Do set aside more of that lovely honeycomb for me. I am already done with the last chunk you brought me, and I shall be disconsolate until I can get more. Its sweetness is a reminder of you. If only, if only, there were some way to erase the distance between us!"

The mention of honeycomb rang a bell for Delphine, in some dim recess of her mind, but try as she might, she could not remember what it was. She moved on.

The next letter was in a different hand, even more beautifully penned, with an earlier date. Delphine scanned down the pages.

"...for my whole life. Weaving is what I loved most in life until now, but that does not mean it will be what I love most in the future. You are the star in my night sky. Say the word, &, I will make the trip to visit you. To see the castle of the Threaded! Most will think that is why I cannot wait. But you know the truth. It is to see my beloved. Has it truly been only weeks since we met? I feel as if I have known you since the world began. I have been talking of nothing but you, &, I daresay my friends are finding me quite tiresome, but I feel I could run across the seas if it meant seeing you again. Only yesterday, I went down to the stockrooms to gather more thread, and I saw the little passageway where we first laid eyes on each other. I am not ashamed to say that I stood for a long moment...."

She skipped through the stack to a letter not in an envelope. Here the same hand was hurried, still elegant, but clearly written in the heat of the moment. Fragments of sentences had been crossed out and rewritten. And it had been folded only once, as if slipped into the stack instead of being sent.

"Darling darling Elodie, please tell me all is safe and all is well. I must ask because of what happened only moments ago with the abbot who is visiting our city. He came to see our workshops, but when he touched my paw, all he could speak of was a terrible danger that will befall me and my loved ones. ~~He kept saying he could not predict the future but I know~~ I believe in the power of premonitions and I refuse to lose you, but where could we go if danger came? Perhaps I can find a secret place for us, or even build a secret place, right inside these very walls! ~~But how would~~ My paws are still shaking and I know none of this makes sense. I will set this draft aside and try again when my nerves have calmed—"

"The letter stops there," said Delphine in frustration. She pawed through the pile, wanting to know what happened.

A low voice came slithering through the air from nowhere. *"What did you say?"*

Delphine gave a little yelp, her ears bone-white. Alexander was staring at the whisper-holes.

She reddened. Of course. The voice was coming from one

of the holes. She was hearing a conversation taking place somewhere else in the building.

"I went to check the room where you took them to rest. They're gone."

"Well, find them!"

Delphine leapt up. "They're looking for us! We need to get back to the infirmary!"

Alexander took the letter and carefully tied it back up with the rest. "We'll take them with us and finish reading later."

Delphine picked up a shawl from the dresser and wrapped it around the bundle of letters. With a few quick knots, the shawl was slung across her shoulder like a bag. "An old trick my mother taught me." She smiled, but the thought of Maman brought a pang to her heart.

She took one last look around, imagining living in these tiny rooms for years, sealed off from the world. What a lonely existence. What had the inhabitants feared would happen? The writer, Maturin, had mentioned a premonition in his letter. Yet the rooms had never been used. Had the prediction never come to pass?

Unless the danger had struck without warning. Perhaps Maturin and Elodie had never even had the chance to reach the hidden rooms that had been so carefully prepared.

The thought sent a shiver down Delphine's tail.

INTERLUDE

Rien gave Elodie one last squeeze for good luck. "I can't believe you're getting married!" He was overflowing with happiness for his old friend, especially after she had reassured him she was remaining at the castle.

"This is where the Threaded have always lived," she had reminded Rien. "Maturin will join me here and travel to his workshop each month. Weaving is his art, the way he creates beauty in this world. I could never ask him to leave that behind. But I won't be lonely when he's there since I'll always have you."

Rien smiled. "You deserve every bit of happiness," he said. "I've never known anyone kinder than you."

Elodie laughed, her nose crinkling. "Don't be silly, Rien! You're far kinder than I am. Why, last week you rescued that caterpillar when it fell into the flour bin. And you gave it a good home. How is Chenille, anyway?"

Rien grinned. "She's been gobbling up the lettuce leaves I've snuck out of the kitchen for her."

Elodie fiddled with the travel cloak wrapped around her shoulders. She was traveling to the city of Maturin's workshop, where she and Maturin were to be wed by the local badger priest. "I'll be back before you know it, and you'll finally get to meet Maturin. I know he'll love you as much as I do."

Rien handed her a chunk of fresh bread from the kitchen. He had carefully wrapped it in a scrap of clean cloth. "So you won't get hungry on your trip."

True to her word, the time passed quickly and soon Elodie returned home with Maturin in tow. Everyone in the kitchen bubbled with gossip about the new couple. Rien was so nervous to meet Maturin that he thought his tail might tie itself into knots. But when Elodie brought her new husband down to their secret little alcove in the tunnels, Maturin swept Rien up into a strong embrace as if they'd known each other all their lives.

"So you're the famous Rien!" said Maturin in a rich baritone. "Elodie is lucky to have as true a friend as you."

"I'm lucky to have Elodie," replied Rien. "She was my friend when I had none at all." He didn't mention that she was still his only friend, that the staff of the kitchen had grown crueler with their bullying as he had grown.

Perhaps Maturin could read some of that on Rien's face, because he clapped the little rat on the back. "You and I shall be best of friends as well, I'm certain of it."

Whenever Maturin had to travel back to the weaving workshop, he would take Rien aside. "Keep Elodie company for me," he always said quietly. "I'm glad she won't be alone while I'm away."

Time passed. Everything was roses and sweet honeycomb. And one day, Elodie told Rien the only thing that could have made him even happier. "We're going to have a baby," she confided. "And we want you to be the godfather."

Rien had never been so thrilled in all his life. All he had ever wanted was to be accepted and loved by those around him, and now he would be part of Elodie's family.

When the baby arrived, Elodie and Maturin carried her down to the secret alcove to meet Rien. He gazed at her in awe, and the baby gazed back solemnly, her tiny nose twitching. "Will she be one of the Threaded, too?" he asked Elodie.

"If her whiskers turn silver in the Ceremony of the Silvering, then she will." Elodie smiled. "Not every child of the Threaded bloodline becomes a Threaded. But I certainly hope so."

Rien held the baby, rocked her, and dandled her on his knee.

"Look at that—Rien's a natural!" Maturin laughed, kissing Elodie on the cheek.

The baby reached up one tiny paw and pulled on Rien's whiskers. He chuckled. "Hello, tiny one," he cooed. "What do you want from Uncle Rien?"

She burbled with delight, and his heart was fuller than it had ever been before. All was finally perfect in his little world.

Chapter 11

Delphine and Alexander stepped back into the abandoned storeroom. Behind them, the tunnel that led to the hidden chambers was dark once again. She let the glow fade from her needle, watching the strange runes carved in the shaft fade as well. Would she ever learn what they meant? *Perhaps when all this is over,* she told herself. She flicked her needle at the pile of stones, and they piled themselves up in front of the doorway until it was blocked once more from sight.

Back upstairs, the guard was no longer at the door of the infirmary room. The two of them tiptoed inside. Julite sat at Ysabeau's bedside, watching their friend sleep. At the sound of their footsteps, Julite jumped, then let out a short laugh.

"You're back!" She passed one paw over her forehead, wiping away the sweat that had appeared.

Delphine was instantly concerned. "What's wrong?"

"I'm worried about . . . travel plans. I don't know if I'll be able to get to the castle in time." She cleared her throat.

"The castle?" Alexander squeaked.

Julite nodded. "The human prince and princess have set a date for their wedding. And the human Duchess of Montrenasse is attending, so we'll be drawing lots to see which mice get to hitch a ride to the castle. I'd do anything to be on that carriage." A twitchy half smile stole across Julite's face.

Delphine coughed loudly. "I was asking about our friends," she said with some rancor.

Julite's expression grew somber. "I sent one of my apprentices for the healer but she hasn't returned. And I dare not send another, not with the rats rampaging through the city streets. Your friend is getting worse. She needs help. Real help."

"And . . . Bearnois?" Delphine could barely bring herself to say the words.

Julite said nothing, merely shook her head. Bearnois was gone.

A pain rose up inside Delphine.

"Without the healer here, I fear that . . ." Julite's voice trailed off. "If only we could send someone else to find him." Her eyes held Delphine in their unblinking gaze.

Delphine stiffened. She wouldn't stand by and watch another one of her friends die. She spun toward the door. "*I'll* get the healer."

Julite was at her side in an instant. "But the rats—"

Delphine moved away from Julite's solicitous paw. "I've got the needle. And I can run and hide if I need to." She looked at Alexander, knowing what he was about to say. "I'm going alone."

"No, you're not." Alexander's eyes were hard. "Ysabeau is my friend, too. I've known her for far longer than you have."

She flushed. How could she have forgotten? "All right."

Julite bit her lip. "It may be easier if she goes alone. Two are twice as likely to draw attention. Alexander, you will be safe here."

But Alexander was already standing at Delphine's side, his paw resting on his sword. "I thank you for your concern, but I have sworn an oath to protect my lady."

Julite sighed. "I'll draw you a map of where the healer's home lies. It's not far, but it's through a dangerous neighborhood. The rats are everywhere now." She shook her head. "Montrenasse-sur-Terre was never like *this*."

✳   ✳   ✳

With Julite's scribbled map in her paw, Delphine stood in the antechamber of the workshop, staring at the front door. The sun had long since set, and she could see nothing but blackness through the little window. Her heart was thumping so hard in her chest, she could barely breathe. She clutched her needle.

Alexander reached out and squeezed her other paw tight. "Are you sure about this?" he whispered.

She nodded. She had to do whatever she could to save Ysabeau.

The moment she stepped outside, an icy gust hit her square in the whiskers. After a few steps down the dark street, she realized she had no idea how far to go before the first turn. Julite's map was rough at best.

Her thoughts were interrupted by dark shadows all around them: rats, emerging swiftly through the swirling flakes. They swarmed toward the two mice, chittering as they came. Delphine and Alexander fled back toward the workshop but the door was locked. They banged frantically.

The tiny window in the door popped open, and Julite's beady eyes appeared. "Sorry, honey. Business is business, and the bounty on your head was too good to resist. Nothing personal." The little window slammed shut. It reopened a moment later. "Oh, and your friend is fine. The healer arrived some time ago and already got her patched up. She's got no reward on *her* head. Your boyfriend would have been fine, too, if he hadn't insisted on tagging along on your fool's errand." The window closed once more. Julite was gone.

The shock lasted only a moment. "Traitor!" Delphine threw herself against the door, pounding in desperation, but it was bolted tight. The dark rage rose inside her, filling her up, overtaking everything else.

Shaking, she turned back to face the rats who were closing in. Her paw flew up, pointing the needle at the closest rat, and lightning lanced out at him. She turned, took aim again. Cold blue fire blazed across the ground, forming a circle around another rat. He screamed, trapped inside the fiery ring. The flames sped across the ground and lapped up the front of an abandoned building on the other side of the street. In an instant, the entire facade was ablaze.

The harsh light of the blue flames cast an unearthly glow across the scene. Alexander went nose to nose with a rat wielding a rusty dagger, parrying and thrusting. He was fast, but the rat was just as quick, and unforgiving.

Even more rats loomed up before her. In terror and rage, she lashed out with the needle. Another blast of fire, even fiercer than the last, flew toward them. The rats turned and ran, straight toward the burning building. But the fire had been eating away at the foundations of the facade, and in that instant, the entire front panel of the building fell on them in a thundering crash.

The wall of blue flame was expanding in every direction. Delphine reached forward with her magic to push it away from herself and toward the rats, but at her touch, it flared up toward the sky. The lash of fire caught her across the paws. She cried out in pain.

Alexander was at her side in an instant. She slumped against his shoulder, feeling the heat on her face. The rats on the far side of the flames were streaming toward the edges.

"Delfie!" He shook her hard. "I can't fight them all. Delphine, I need you!"

Head lolling, she tried to connect with the magic again, but the pain was eating away at the edges of her mind. She couldn't focus. There was no way the magic could break through.

"I can't. . . ." She fell, her last bit of strength focused on keeping the needle in her pained grip. Alexander pulled her up, and they ran as he half carried, half pushed her. The buildings on the far side of the street were all now on fire, their facades crumbling into the street. Some of the rats were caught beneath the rubble, but most still pursued them.

"We just have to reach the town gates," Alexander panted as they ran. Delphine remembered faintly that Cornichonne was supposed to be waiting for them. They turned corners blindly, until they spotted the top of a guard tower above the roofline. "There!" They emerged onto the main thoroughfare. To their left loomed the gates of the human city, closed and bolted until morning. To their right, more rats were spilling from alleyways. And there next to the doors of the gate, curled up atop a stack of grain sacks, was a sleeping Cornichonne.

Alexander squeaked as loudly as he could. There was no point in worrying about stealth anymore. Cornichonne's eyes popped open. In another instant, she leapt down beside them.

"Where are Ysabeau and Bearnois?"

"Never mind about that." Alexander shoved Delphine onto Cornichonne's back. Was the shawl still tied across her shoulder? Ignoring the pain, she turned to see her needle safe in Alexander's grasp.

"Are they all right?" The cat's voice was rough.

Alexander scrambled on, looping one paw around Delphine and getting a firm hold on Cornichonne's fur with the other. "I'll explain later. We have to get out of here." The rats were headed straight for them, their sharp yellow teeth gleaming in the light of the street torches. Cornichonne turned and dashed through the hole in the city wall.

Outside the gates, the snow was blinding. The cat twitched one ear. "I know where we can go."

"Take us." Delphine felt Alexander leaning over her, protecting her from the worst of the wind, as Cornichonne bounded into the storm. In another moment, there was nothing to see but white.

MIDNIGHT PACED THE LONELY HALLS of his fortress. He knew these halls better than the back of his paw. Every hidden staircase, every secret passage: he knew them all.

The fortress was nearly empty. Only a few of his most loyal minions remained. He had sent the rest out across the kingdom to hunt for the mouse with the needle. And Valentine had disappeared with no explanation at all. At least he still had Mezzo. Faithful Mezzo. She was a little too intelligent for her own good, and not nearly bloodthirsty enough for his taste, but he knew she would never betray him. She couldn't. He had seen to that.

He pulled his black velvet cloak tighter against the chill of the old stones. He was always cold now. A faint memory floated up from somewhere, the feeling of golden sunshine falling on his ears and paws, warming his blood. That had been so long ago, before he had gained his powers.

Through the hall windows, he saw the sun hanging high in the sky, exactly as it had every day for the last hundred years. It was laughing at him, he thought. Laughing at how he was a prisoner in his own home.

Had it truly been more than a hundred years since he had been transformed? A hundred years since he had been saved from death and healed of his wounds? That transformation had given him a strength he'd never known. With it coursing through his veins, he had stumbled into glory, scheming to take over the entire kingdom— to lead his troops across the land, razing and burning as they went.

That was a century ago, and yet he remembered it as if it were yesterday. . . .

The successful ransacking of the fortress. The purge of the unworthy inhabitants. The next morning, a hundred years ago, he had decided to strike out in search of more rats to join his army. Flush with success, he left the fortress before dawn. He walked toward the edge of the forest, savoring the fresh morning air. Slowly, the rays of the sun broke over the horizon.

He began to feel a strange pain in his legs as he walked. At first, it was a dull ache, but it grew with each passing minute. Then fresh pain stabbed through his chest. He tore open his cloak and scrabbled at his fur, but there was no wound. Only the pale scars that had been left when his wounds sealed themselves.

Another wave of pain shot up his back, and he stumbled, falling to his knees. It felt as if he were being pummeled from all directions. The sun had climbed over the horizon, and its bright light poured down on him.

Was the sunlight doing this to him? He didn't know, and didn't want to find out. Anything was better than enduring this pain for a moment longer. He turned and dragged himself back to the fortress.

Once he slipped inside the doors, the pain began to lessen, fading away like a terrible dream. He laid one trembling paw on the stone wall. Perhaps it wasn't the sun at all. Perhaps he simply couldn't leave the fortress. But no matter the reason, he was trapped.

This was the first time he'd wondered if the needles were more than trophies of war to be displayed on a wall. The Threaded had used those needles to summon powerful magic. Perhaps he could harness that magic to free himself.

Thus was born a fruitless hope. But year after year had passed, and try as he might, he couldn't wring a drop of magic from those damnable needles. He grew ever more hopeless, until he was forced to believe that perhaps the eleven needles he possessed were useless without the twelfth. And the twelfth was nowhere to be found. He would be trapped in this godforsaken fortress forever. . . .

A sound startled him back to the present, and he realized it was the sound of his own ragged breath. He continued down the hall, still grimacing at that bright orb hanging in the sky.

Dizziness swept over him. Why was his body failing around him? Was eternity forsaking him after all? Every day he felt weaker than he ever had before. He stumbled and his ankle twisted beneath him. He swore, struggling to remain upright. He was coming apart at the seams.

He snarled. Once he got that twelfth needle, he would rain down terror on the kingdom until every last mouse was dead. He had a century of fury to unleash.

Chapter 12

Cornichonne chirped loudly in the cold air, then paused and cocked her ears. She had been making this strange sound all afternoon. They'd left the city of Montrenasse-sur-Terre far behind them the night before and slept under the cover of an old tree. But now, after they'd traveled in a straight line all morning, the cat was wandering in circles in the snow.

"Where are we?" asked Delphine woozily. She kept fading in and out of consciousness from the pain of her burned paws. Had

Alexander strapped her onto the cat's back so she wouldn't fall off, or were those his strong arms wrapped around her?

Alexander smoothed back her whiskers. "We're going somewhere safe."

Delphine wasn't sure if she believed him. Even through the pain, she could feel the cat wandering aimlessly.

Alexander leaned forward. "Uh . . . Cornichonne? Are you sure you know where you're going?"

Cornichonne nodded. "Yiss. We're going to see the bats. Their cave is right around here somewhere. But everything looks the same under all this snow."

"The *bats*?" repeated Alexander.

"They're my friends." She chirped again, swiveling her ears. "I'm calling them now."

Through half-open eyes, Delphine saw Alexander pass a paw over his forehead. She struggled to form a sentence. "Cats and bats can talk together over distance? S'that true?"

He shrugged, then turned back to the cat. "How exactly are you talking to them?"

"Echolocation," replied Cornichonne.

As if on cue, a fluttering silhouette appeared above them, moving through the low-hanging fog. Cornichonne stopped in her tracks, her ears perking up.

"Bats," she said once more.

Delphine felt her head dipping even lower, her breath coming in shallow pants. Alexander's arms tightened around her. "Whatever we're going to do, we have to do it quickly. Delphine needs our help."

※ ※ ※

Delphine felt cool fingertips on her head, gentle and sure. She blinked. Where was she? Then she remembered how Julite had sold her out, the swirl of blue flames, Cornichonne's plan to find the bats. She moaned.

A voice came from nearby, as soft as the touch on her brow. "You have the winter fever, little one," somebody said. Were they talking to her? She raised her head and her vision began to spin. The blue flames flared around her once more. Everything went black.

She was back home again, following the silver thread through the halls, still trying to find the end. It was leading her somewhere, she was sure of that, but she could see nothing ahead in the dark.

The next time she woke, her head had cleared. She realized she was inside a cave. Someone had tucked her into a cozy little bed with a thistledown mattress. Most of the small room was bare, but the natural stone walls were scrubbed clean and the ground was well swept. It made her think of the cellar back at Château Desjardins. She remembered how Cinderella would sweep it daily, rain or shine. It felt like so long ago.

Delphine slipped out of the bed and found she was dressed in a linen nightgown. Her clothes sat on a chair, carefully cleaned and folded. Her needle leaned against the wall nearby.

Her paws were wrapped in bandages, thick but soft. She tried to peer underneath. A jolt of pain lanced through her as she tugged on the wrappings.

Steadying herself, she turned her attention to her clothes. Somebody had repaired all of the tears and worn spots they had suffered over the last few weeks. She carefully slipped into her underdress and girdle, then awkwardly tied her overskirt. The bandages made everything difficult.

Alexander knocked at the door, a wry smile on his face. "We really must stop meeting like this."

She smiled back, uncertain. "What do you mean?"

"Oh, just . . . you recovering in a strange room, me trying to reassure you that everything will be all right." He gave a nervous laugh. Then he noticed that she was fiddling with her bandages. He walked over and gently took her paws in his. "Delfie, what you did with that blue fire . . . it could have killed us."

"But it *saved* us."

He narrowed his eyes. "This time."

"I don't understand, Alexander. You know who I have to defeat. How can I succeed if I don't have enough power? That wall of fire—"

"The one that nearly killed you."

"—could be the thing that defeats Midnight."

He nodded. "Possibly. But what if it isn't?"

"Then the rats win, and the kingdom is lost forever. Is that what you want to hear? That the rats could win?" She broke down, covering her face with her bandaged paws.

Then Alexander was at her side, holding her tight. "You won't fail, Delfie. I'll help you."

"*How,* Alexander?"

"I don't know." Alexander stood for a long time, his arms around her. Delphine leaned against him. "I don't know."

Delphine looked at her needle leaning against the wall. "I need to get stronger."

✳ ✳ ✳

Alexander offered to introduce her to their hosts, but she felt like she should meet them on her own. "You've already done more than enough," she insisted. She reached out to smooth his whiskers, then caught herself and blushed.

He grinned. "Go on, then. You never did need anyone else to speak for you."

She tiptoed down a dark corridor carved through the stone. For a moment she was in blackness, but then the passage curved and an archway appeared. A gentle glow came from the other side, so steady it couldn't be from a candle.

Walking through the archway, she found herself in a much larger cave. Raw gemstones studded the stone walls. The center of the room was taken up by a huge glass bottle from the human world. It had been converted into a terrarium, populated by contented lightning bugs. They glowed softly as they rested on the branches. It was a lovely sight.

A polite cough drew her attention. She looked upward to see several brown bats hanging comfortably from the ceiling.

"You've awoken," said one. "So the winter fever has finally let you go." With a creaky outstretch of her wings, she fluttered down to the floor. "I am Claudette Bonnenuit. Welcome to our home. You were in poor shape, Mademoiselle Delphine. The snow is still dangerous outside for one with injuries as severe as yours. You must all remain with us until it is safe to leave the cave on paw again."

Delphine had seen no windows yet, or doors to the outside world. "Is it still snowing?"

Another bat spoke up, still hanging from the ceiling. "Yes, ever since you arrived, and likely to keep on for at least a week."

Claudette beckoned to her. "Come and see for yourself, little wingless bat."

They traveled down a long passageway, through more cave rooms, and finally came to a high, narrow space where window slits overlooked the ground outside. Delphine gasped.

The world had been transformed. A white blanket stretched as far as the eye could see, and more snow was coming down with no sign of stopping.

She looked back at Claudette. "If you'll let us stay, we'll do what we can to earn our keep."

Claudette smiled, her filmy eyes warm. "Alexander told me you would say that."

Chapter 13

Delphine and Alexander asked for directions to the cellar where Cornichonne was resting. The network of caves the bats inhabited was huge. "Take one of our lightning bugs to light your way," instructed Claudette. She handed Delphine its spiderweb leash. The lightning bug floated happily between them.

The tunnels twisted and turned, but after a while, the mice found themselves at the entrance to a cave much larger than all the previous ones. It had a naturally arched ceiling and a cozy dirt floor. A large, round ball of gray fur lay snoring in one corner.

Delphine squealed and ran to her friend's side. She covered Cornichonne's damp nose with kisses.

The cat blinked the sleep away, jolting up. "You're all better!"

Delphine held up her bandaged paws. "Not entirely," she admitted. "But much better than I would have been if you hadn't gotten us out of there."

Cornichonne peered at her. "What happened?"

As Delphine took a deep breath, unsure where to begin, Alexander wrapped his arms around her. "The rats attacked and Delphine fought them off with fire."

The cat's eyes widened. "You're a hero," she snuffled.

"No, I'm not," Delphine protested, her lips trembling. "I couldn't save Bearnois. He—" The words caught in her throat.

There was a pause. Then Cornichonne spoke in a low murmur. "I couldn't feel him anymore, after you went into the tunnels under the city." She sniffed as a tear slid down her whisker. "I wanted to be wrong."

"We all did," Alexander said. "At least Ysabeau is on the mend. She's safe. Julite had no grudge against her."

Delphine nodded miserably. She couldn't forgive Julite for betraying her to the rats, but she understood how desperate the mouse must have been to secure protection for her loved ones.

Cornichonne shifted. "So did you find any clues in the city?" she asked, clearly trying to change the subject.

"Well, we did find the tapestry workshop." Delphine raised her head. "That's where all this happened. And we found letters, sent to and from one of the Threaded." Just then, a fear struck her. "Alexander, the letters! Did we lose them?"

"Weren't they in your room when you woke up?"

"I—I'm not sure. Wait here." Delphine ran back up the passages, burst into the bedroom, and gasped in relief. Yes, there lay the scarf, still tied around the bundle of letters, hanging from the foot of the bed. She snatched it up and headed back down to the cellar.

"Here they are," she breathed when she returned. She tried to unknot the scarf, but the bandages on her paws made her clumsy. Alexander took the bundle and unwrapped it.

"Most are written by someone named Élodie, who must have been a member of the Threaded," Delphine explained. "I think I saw that name in the tapestries at Château Trois Arbres."

Cornichonne leaned in to look. But as she let out an interested whuffle, the topmost letter fluttered onto the dirt floor. The cat squeaked, laying her head on her paws in mortification, as Alexander ran to grab it and reknot the letters into the scarf for safekeeping.

"It's all right," Delphine consoled. Suddenly she noticed how frostbitten the cat's toes were.

"You need healing balm for your toe pads," Delphine said. The letters could wait. She wasn't going to let her friend suffer.

✳ ✳ ✳

Delphine and Alexander visited Cornichonne every day to rub healing balm on her frostbitten toes. The balm soothed Delphine's paws as well. Each evening, she returned to her little bedroom and under the glow of a friendly lightning bug, read more of the letters. But there were no clues about her ancestor, nor anything else that helped unlock more of the needle's magic. Discouraged, she read less and less each night until soon she had put the letters aside altogether.

The family of bats was amiable and energetic in the winter, when there was so much nighttime to enjoy and so little daylight to avoid. Delphine finally screwed up the courage to ask why they had the lightning bugs if they were bats and loved the dark, and Claudette laughed.

"The night is always a little cozier with some stars, don't you think? And our dark cave is happier with the glow of our friends."

Since they were stuck there until both Delphine's and Cornichonne's paws mended, Delphine found ways to busy herself. She couldn't bear to be a burden, hearing Maman's voice in her head: *"Idle paws get nothing done."* So when she found out about a side-cave filled with acorns, she taught the bats how to grind them into flour and bake sweet, flaky biscuits. She tended to the lightning bugs, learning how to feed and groom them. She swept the stone corridors, picturing her mother sweeping the front doorstep of Château Desjardins, where Delphine had been left so long ago.

As soon as Delphine's paws had healed enough, she got to work on stitching together fabric covers that could lace up around Cornichonne's paws so the cat wouldn't suffer frostbite again. She coated them with wax to make them waterproof and stuffed them with a thick lining of feathery down. Pleased with her work, she made two smaller sets for herself and Alexander as well.

On a chilly afternoon, she stumbled across an old pair of human boots, lying long abandoned in one of the bats' many annex caves. An idea popped into her mind: with the leather, she could construct a proper saddle. The bats were pleased as dandelion punch for Delphine to make use of the boots.

"There are treasures of all sorts scattered throughout our caves," said Claudette. "And not only the treasures of bats. Caves have been used for safekeeping since time immemorial. Who knows what hidden treasures still lie out there in the peaks of the Peltinore mountains?"

As she gnawed and stitched at the shoe leather, Delphine felt like she was back in her element. She had spent many happy hours at Cinderella's château, learning from other mice how to make the most of every little human castoff. Now she repurposed each piece of leather, using the buckled ankle straps to hold the saddle in place, and fashioning the leftover panels into pockets. She knew they would have to carry all their own food when they set out again. They wouldn't be digging up acorns or picking more berries until the spring if the snow kept going the way it had been.

Alexander helped her settle the whole contraption onto Cornichonne's back. Delphine kept fussing, running from side to side, loosening this strap and readjusting that one. "Are you sure it's comfortable enough?" she asked the cat over and over, her face crinkled with worry.

Finally, Cornichonne put out one paw and stopped Delphine. "It's perfect," she snuffed. "I love the little saddlebags."

Day after day, the snow outside blew so hard it looked like it was falling sideways. Soon Delphine had mended everything she could lay her paws on, including anything that could be fixed with the magic of her needle. One evening, she and Alexander were sitting with Cornichonne in her cellar cave, trying to keep themselves entertained. Delphine began braiding the fur between Cornichonne's toes.

The cat was not as enthusiastic about the activity as Delphine was. "Uh, Delphine . . ." she said finally, tucking her paws underneath her body as she did, "can we do something else now? How about those letters you found?"

"There's nothing in them." Delphine eyed Cornichonne's whiskers and wondered if the cat would let her curl them.

"But maybe we can read together?"

Delphine got the sense Cornichonne was trying to distract her, but she headed up to her room anyway and retrieved the stack. She supposed she could spend a few hours making a little more progress through the love notes she still hadn't read.

As soon as she untied the scarf, the cat was snuffling at the papers again. "What's this?" Cornichonne poked one claw at the middle of the pile.

Delphine flipped forward. All the envelopes looked the same to her, but Cornichonne had her nose glued to one in particular. It was farther down in the stack—one Delphine hadn't reached before. She slipped one claw under the flap of the envelope. The smell of vellum and sand wafted out as she removed a thin sheaf of papers. She gazed at them as Alexander leaned over her shoulder.

The sheets were filled with minuscule handwriting. A column of illuminated illustration ran down the left side of each page, brimming with beautiful hand-drawn details. Every page featured a different theme within the column: birds, fish, stars, clouds. One included delicious-looking honeycombs. Another was topped with a golden crown.

To the right of the illuminated columns ran rows and rows of carefully inked text. These were definitely not love letters like the other pages. These held documentation: lists of names, dates, events.

Delphine studied the page in her paw. Her heart beat faster. There weren't only drawings in the columns. A series of runes were worked into the swirls. She glanced at another page. A different set of runes in each column, in a different order.

She ran her eyes over the runes again, confirming what she already knew. These symbols were familiar. As a child, she had gone to sleep every night gazing at them. . . .

She stared at Alexander, her eyes huge, then pulled out her needle and placed it on the ground, breathless. Next to it, she laid the page with the column of hearts.

"Look." Her paws were trembling as she pointed. The first rune on the page was the first rune on her needle. Same for the second, and the third, and the fourth. . . . The entire series was identical, rune for rune, on the sheet that lay before them.

"By the whiskers of Rhapso," Alexander whispered in awe. "It's the inscription from your needle, repeated on the pages."

"Only this page." She was looking at the columns on the other pages again. "The set of runes on that page with the hearts is the only one that exactly matches the needle. The other ones are . . . each in a different order."

They spread all the pages back out again. Delphine ground her teeth, wishing she had more information. If only she hadn't lost all her papers with the song lyrics from the music school when they had fled Château Trois Arbres.

"Cornichonne!" She turned to the cat as a thought struck her. "Will you sing those songs you always sing on the road? The ones about the Threaded?"

The cat began to croon in her nasal growl. Her soothing tones wrapped around Delphine as she listened, but there were no answers in the lyrics. There was still something she was missing, something right in front of her on these twelve sheets of paper.

Twelve pages for twelve Threaded. Could it be that easy?

The old nursery rhyme popped into her head. As the cat finished her tune, Delphine spoke softly, the words so familiar that she could recite them in her sleep.

The First rides the wind. The Second walks on light.
The Third bends the waves. The Fourth moves with might.
The Fifth sings with birds. The Sixth paints the sky.
The Seventh writes the song. The Eighth draws the eye.
The Ninth touches stars. The Tenth sweetens tart.
The Eleventh reads the dreams. And the Twelfth knows the heart.

Alexander's whiskers trembled in excitement as she spoke. "Birds! And stars!" He grabbed excitedly at two of the sheets. "Delfie, that's it!" He looked over the rest of them. "Say it again, Delfie? What were the other symbols?"

"*Wind . . .*" she began, leaning in next to him. There it was, now that she was looking for it, plain as day. One of the illuminated columns was wrapped in a long breath of air, coming out of a stylized cloud at the top with a mouse's face.

Alexander moved that page far to the left. "Let's put them in order."

"The second one is *light*." She wasn't sure about that one. She kept going. "Next is . . . *waves*." That was easy. They placed the page with fish swimming through the column to the right of the first page. The fish in the illustrations were so realistic that Delphine caught Cornichonne licking her lips.

She repeated the rhyme in her head. *". . . moves with might. Might?"* She wrinkled her nose, and Alexander shrugged.

She kept going. *"Birds* and *sky*. We have the birds already."

He nodded and positioned the page with the birds alongside the others, then pointed at a page showing a column of silvery clouds.

"Yes!" she agreed. "That has to be *sky*!"

"What's next?" He was studying a page decorated with a column made of stone.

She had to think. *"The Seventh writes the song.* Musical notes?" Sure enough, one column had what could be musical chords from a certain angle. "And then . . . *The Eighth draws the eye.*"

"This one." Alexander laid down a page featuring winking eyes of all colors. They now had eight pages laid out in front of them. He shuffled the remaining. "Say the last four."

Delphine recited carefully. *"Stars.* You have that already.

Tart . . . I don't know. Wait! Maybe the one with the honey-comb? *The Tenth sweetens tart?*"

Alexander grinned. "Agreed." He placed it in sequence with the other pages.

"*Dreams* and *heart*. That's all that's left. And obviously that one is the heart." She moved the page with the heart-themed column into place. Three pages remained—one with the phases of the moon, one with stones, and one with a gold crown.

Cornichonne gazed at the one with the crown. "Pretty sunrise."

Delphine crowed. "Cornichonne, you're right! That isn't a crown, that's the sun rising over the horizon! So that must be the page for *light*."

Two pages remained. "Stone could symbolize might. Strong and unyielding?" She shifted the other pages to place it into the correct order.

"But . . ." They were left with the column showing the phases of the moon. "Does the moon represent *dreams?*" She pursed her lips. It didn't seem to fit, not the way the rest had.

Cornichonne leaned in even closer. "My dreams are like little fluffy thoughts that float in and out of my head when I'm asleep."

Delphine nodded, realizing that she thought of her dreams the same way. Like clouds, floating above her head. She picked up the page with the clouds and replaced it with the page of the moon. "The moon lives in the *sky*," she said. Then in the one remaining empty spot, she carefully laid down the page with the clouds. "*The Eleventh reads the dreams.*" They were done.

The twelve pages stretched across the ground above the needle, as long as its shaft. She gazed again at the last page, at the illuminated column that had first caught her eye, emblazoned with hearts. The page with the runes that perfectly matched those on her needle. Hearts, for the Twelfth.

"It was right in front of me all along," she whispered, picking up her needle. "It's not just a nursery rhyme. It's who they *were*, all twelve of them. Every one of those twelve lines described the powers of one of the Threaded. And these runes . . . they wrote about their abilities in their own secret language." She ran a trembling paw over the markings on her needle. "I'm sure that if the other needles still existed, they would have inscriptions, too. And they'd match the runes on the eleven other pages."

Alexander put his arm around her shoulder and squeezed her so close she could feel his warm breath on her cheek. "You figured it out." His whiskers tickled hers.

She wondered if some part of her had known which needle it was, deep down, ever since she had first felt the magic in her paws. She remembered the awe that had flowed through her heart that night on the river, as she gazed up at the full moon. She had been drawn deeper into the magic as her heartfelt passion to complete her quest had grown. And in the last few weeks, the hatred for Midnight that burned in her heart had been driving the magic to dangerous places.

She ran her eyes over the runes on her needle. It was so simple to read, now that she knew what it said.

The Twelfth knows the heart.

VALENTINE CAPERED ACROSS THE FROZEN crust of the snow, humming a pleasant little tune. Why on earth had she stayed with King Midnight for so long? True, at the start it had seemed like a fun diversion, and his pompous airs had amused her. But the humor had worn away. She wished she had been able to avoid Mezzo and get her claws on those eleven needles, though nothing was better than being out in the wintry world, with nobody to answer to but herself.

She wondered if Midnight had noticed yet that she was gone. Probably not. It always took him forever to figure what was actually going on in his fortress. Had he even realized that Snurleau was missing until she herself had mentioned it? She chuckled snidely. What a weevil.

Pausing to listen by a tree trunk, Valentine peeled back the bark with her sharp claws, and was rewarded with a handful of grubs. Lovely little snack. She popped them into her mouth one by one, savoring their squishy bodies, then continued on. She didn't need a destination. She knew that if she kept heading south, eventually she'd find her way out of Peltinore. What lay below the kingdom? Nothing got her heart beating faster than the promise of a brand-new adventure.

Valentine was passing a massive outcropping of rocks when a strangely familiar scent tickled her nose. She stood perfectly still, waiting for another whiff, and was rewarded. Somehow it was coming from within the rocks.

Why did she know that smell? The phantom pain of devilthorn swarmed over her. She twitched. The little gray mouse with the needle! Valentine recalled how she and Snurleau had tracked down the mouse, only to discover she was accompanied by a drooling monster. That cat-beast had chased them straight into a forest filled with devilthorn.

The ermine shuddered. It had taken her weeks of soaking in a mud bath to get all the poison out of her wounds. Snurleau had decided to run back home to Midnight. Stupid Snurleau. He always put far too much trust in the rat king. Valentine never made that mistake.

A cunning plan dropped itself into her lap. She had seen with her own eyes how much power that little gray mouse could summon with her needle. And based on Midnight's reaction whenever the needle was mentioned, Valentine had also deduced how frightened Midnight was of that power (though he did an excellent job of hiding it from the rest of his troops). What if the mouse and Midnight were to come face-to-face? Wouldn't it be positively delightful if Valentine were able to arrange Midnight's defeat from afar? She wouldn't need to get a single one of her own snow-white paws dirty.

And if the mouse failed? If Midnight destroyed her and got his claws on the needle? Valentine shrugged. *She* wouldn't lose anything either way. But at least she could have a good laugh, knowing she had brought even more trouble to Midnight's doorstep.

After secreting her travel bag inside an old stump and rubbing dirt into her fur to look more bedraggled, she began to climb up the rock outcropping. She nosed out the entrance after a few minutes. It was tight, but she managed to wriggle her way inside.

Valentine found herself in a plain but pleasant cave, the floor swept clean and a bat hanging from the ceiling. She cleared her throat loudly.

The bat half opened one eye. Terror swept across its features. "Invader!" it cried, dropping from the ceiling and fluttering around the room wildly. "Ermine invader!" In an instant, a half-dozen more bats had dashed into the room. With them came two mice. One was russet-colored with a dagger in his paw. The other was the gray mouse Valentine remembered, and sure enough, she was clutching an oversize needle.

Valentine suppressed a smile, making sure her face appeared mournful and beaten down. She dropped to her knees and raised her forepaws. "I come in peace! I wish to right my wrongs."

The bats screeched at her, ready to attack, but the gray mouse put out a paw and they fell back. Then the mouse approached warily, her head held high. Valentine had to admit she had a lot of gumption. "I recognize you," the mouse said. She had the needle pointed straight at Valentine's throat. "Do you work for Midnight?"

"I did," moaned Valentine, "until it all became too much. I saw the error of my ways. I couldn't stand by and be party to all that bloodshed." She pretended to cry and even managed to produce some real tears.

"Why should I believe you?" asked the mouse, but Valentine could hear her voice softening.

"I can offer you no proof. But perhaps I can appease my guilty soul and right my wrongs."

"You said that already!" piped up the russet mouse. Valentine took the opportunity to wring her paws together and emit a few loud sniffles.

"I see now how evil Midnight is," continued Valentine. "He cannot be allowed to live. Someone must step forward to save us all." She paused, letting realization wash over her face. "Someone like *you.*"

She was rewarded with a sharp inhale of breath from the little gray mouse. Something had awakened in the mouse's eyes, as if Valentine's words had struck a deep chord.

She believes, crowed Valentine to herself. *The weapon has been charged. Now to point it in the right direction.*

"Go east, to the river, and follow it north!" She made sure she sounded like she was babbling only semicomprehensibly. She knew perfectly well that if she was too clear, the mouse would assume it was a trap. "Follow the river until you hear the pounding. The pounding!" She clutched her head, swaying from side to side. "Oh, it still burns inside my skull!" *Overly histrionic?* she wondered. Perhaps, but she was having too much fun to care.

"Follow the river north?" repeated the mouse. Her whiskers quivered.

"North, to the pounding, and then through the wall . . ." Valentine made herself trail off. "I've said too much already!" she cried. Before the mouse could ask any more questions, she leapt up and dashed back in the direction she had come.

"Find Midnight!" she cried over her shoulder as she ran. "Slay him! Midnight must die!"

With that, Valentine wormed her way back out through the hole and down to the base of the outcropping. Finally, she let herself erupt into quiet laughter. It had all been too perfect. The look on the gray mouse's face, the improvised line about the pounding . . . She retrieved her travel bag, still chuckling, and continued southward. If the mouse somehow managed to make her way to Midnight and destroy him, then Valentine could return at her leisure and destroy the little mouse in turn. And if not? No matter.

Still giggling, she vanished from sight, her white fur blending seamlessly into the snow.

tHe MimoLette mooon

Chapter 14

"*Midnight must die.*" The ermine's words hammered inside Delphine's head. She didn't want to believe it; she had been hoping that he could simply be stripped of his power somehow. But she knew in her heart that it was true. Midnight was too great a threat to the kingdom to be allowed to live.

Another question nagged at her. How could the ermine possibly know that Delphine was strong enough to do it? For that matter, could Delphine believe *anything* that the ermine had to say? That ermine had tried to kill her. It was only thanks to Cornichonne's intervention that she had failed. Now she wanted them to believe that she had repented?

And what about her insistence on giving Delphine directions to Midnight's lair? Resheathing her needle, Delphine turned to Alexander for his thoughts.

"Bit of a shock to see her here," he remarked. "I can't blame her for looking distraught, though. I imagine fleeing from Midnight's employ would be terrifying enough to drive anyone half-mad."

"So you believed her?"

"Well . . ." He pursed his lips. "I once met a fox who had spent the first half of her life tearing the throats out of garden voles. But one day she noticed how beautiful the voles' gardens were. She's been a gardener ever since."

Delphine raised an eyebrow.

"Lovely topiaries she does."

"Does she trim the topiaries by fang or by claw?" one of the bats piped up.

"Alexander." Delphine was determined to get this conversation back on track. "Do we trust that ermine or not?"

"I vote we do," he said with good cheer. "We were planning to head north anyway, weren't we? We'll simply go east first until we hit the river. North is north, in the end."

Delphine nodded, agreeing with his logic. "It's decided."

And now that she had specific directions to follow, she felt the urge to get started. They had already rested for far too long.

Her paws throbbed with a little twinge of pain, as if to remind her they were still healing. But there were more important things to worry about. How much destruction had Midnight's rats inflicted on the kingdom while she had been in the bats' cave? She whispered the last line of the nursery rhyme, the line engraved on her needle: *"The Twelfth knows the heart."* She still didn't know exactly what that meant, but she did know what her own heart was telling her: to set out in search of Midnight once more.

It was quick work to pack up their belongings, and then they said their good-byes. Delphine was beginning to feel as if all she did was make friends and leave them behind. She hugged the whole Bonnenuit clan one by one, Claudette longest of all.

"You saved me," she said to Claudette. "You saved all of us. I'll never be able to thank you enough."

Claudette hugged her back, her leathery wings wrapping entirely around Delphine. "Nonsense, little wingless bat. Cornichonne has helped us many times in the past. We were simply repaying the favor."

The snow was even deeper now than when they had arrived, but there was a solid crust of ice across the top. Cornichonne put out a tentative paw, confirming it could hold her weight, then knelt for them to clamber up onto her back. Then with a delicate tread, Cornichonne set off.

Delphine waved good-bye until she couldn't see the cave mouth anymore.

The ermine's words followed her in a silent refrain. *Midnight must die.* Beneath her heavy travel cloak, Delphine clenched her paws. It was time to find King Midnight and end his reign. Forever.

By midafternoon, two mice weren't feeling so comfortable in the new saddle. Finally, they stopped to take a break. The trees around them were bare, the sky flat and gray. The mice slid from the cat's back onto the snowy ground, legs stiff and sore.

Delphine sniffed the cold air. They had stopped in a naturally formed hollow. Large rocks lay between the widespread trees, helping to slow the biting wind. "Let's set up camp here," she said finally.

"In the middle of the afternoon?" Alexander was nonplussed.

Delphine began to break small, dry twigs from a nearby branch. "We're going to need to ease back into riding for so long every day, and I should spend some time practicing with the needle again now that my paws are finally healing."

She stacked up the twigs and dug out a pinch of dried lichen from one of the pockets on Cornichonne's new saddle. With a flick of her needle, the lichen tinder flamed up. Soon the twigs were crackling gently.

Alexander and Cornichonne needed no further encouragement. They curled up into the lee of the rocks, but despite the heat of the flames, it was still brutally cold.

Delphine watched the woodsmoke rising up toward the sky, carrying away most of their warmth with it. *If only there were some way to capture all that heat*, she thought. An idea struck. She had been able to create a glass roof once to protect all three of them from the rain, inspired by gossip about the mysterious human princess and her glass slippers. If magic could transform glass into shoes and roofs, then why not a wall?

Using the needle, she drew a magical line around the clearing, large enough to encompass all three of them with the twigfire in the center. Slowly the snow on the ground crystallized, turning into glass where the line touched it. The crystals grew taller, rising up into the air. In another instant, a tall glass wall curved around them like a dome, open at the top so the smoke could escape. The air was already getting warmer inside.

"Ooh!" snuffled Cornichonne with pleasure. She uncurled, and stretched out her legs indulgently.

"What are you planning now?" asked Alexander, snuggled up against the cat.

Delphine stepped to the doorway of the glass dome, and pulled her cloak tight against the cold. "I'm going to go practice my magic."

Alexander's brow furrowed. "That's all fine and good, but

what about the bigger plan? We still haven't learned anything new about Midnight, or if he has any weaknesses." Worry had crept into his voice.

Delphine shrugged. "Even if he does have an Achilles paw, that won't be enough if I'm not strong enough to take advantage of it."

"True," he replied, his voice quiet.

She waited for a moment, but he said nothing more. So she turned and left them inside the cozy glass dome.

As Delphine searched for a good place to practice, she tried to focus on the runes: *The Twelfth knows the heart.* But the memory that kept bubbling up was of the first time she had summoned the blue lightning, that night in the tapestry hall of Château Trois Arbres. What had happened to trigger that? Philomène had just told her about the slaughter of the Threaded by the rats, and Delphine had been hit by a wave of anger. Her hatred for the rats had flowed into the needle and appeared as blue lightning. *That* had been the feeling of true power.

She wandered through the trees, thinking back even further in her adventure, to the night on the skiff when she had first unlocked the magic. The moonlight had somehow flowed *through* her, unwinding from her paws and through the needle like thread unspooling. But that had been raw magic, out of her control. This new blue magic was harsh and spiky, channeling her wrath and hate. This she could control.

Delphine took a deep breath and thought of the rats, letting hateful thoughts rise up inside her. When her paws were tingling and the needle was shuddering in her grasp, she aimed at a bare tree branch. A bolt of the cold lightning erupted from the needle, shattering the branch into splinters. Little blue sparks fell, sizzling as they hit the frozen ground. She aimed again and again, exploding branch after branch, the lightning growing stronger each time.

It was terrifying but exhilarating, because it meant she had more power and could fight that much harder. With a concentrated swirling twist of her wrist, she managed to re-create the wall of flame she had summoned in Montrenasse-sur-Terre. The flames circled a nearby tree and shot up the trunk, snatching hungrily at branches as they went. The cold blue light seared the dark sky overhead, as bright as if a full moon had suddenly appeared.

Delphine snapped back to reality. The rats! With the blue fire burning as brightly as it was, she might as well be perched at the top of a tree, yelling at the top of her lungs to draw their attention. The rage fell away from her in an instant, leaving her drenched in a cold sweat. The flames evaporated from the tree as well. Livid burns scarred the trunk, but the fire— and the light it cast—was gone.

She sank to the icy ground, shaking. Was she losing control? Losing sight of what mattered? No. Come what may, she had to save the citizens of the kingdom. If she was going to kill Midnight, she would need every ounce of power she could summon, no matter the cost to herself.

As she returned to the glass dome around their campsite, she could see Alexander and Cornichonne inside, curled up together. They were singing a quiet duet that barely reached her ears where she stood outside the entrance. She suddenly felt very alone.

Alexander's head popped up as she entered. "Delfie! You look half-frozen. Come get warm." He scurried over and wrapped his warm cloak around her. It melted away some of the grief inside, but she still couldn't meet his eyes. The fact that she would have to *kill* Midnight in order to end things was becoming all too real. What made it even worse was that she wasn't able to bring herself to tell Alexander.

$$* \quad * \quad *$$

They finally reached a river, exactly as Valentine had said. It was wide, but flowing so quietly under its mantle of ice that they didn't even know it was there until they were almost on top of it.

"The ermine's been right so far," pointed out Alexander, and Delphine had to agree.

They spent the night inside an empty, rotting tree trunk nearby. The bats had filled the saddle pockets with dried meal-worms from their storeroom. Cornichonne popped them into her mouth like little candies, crunching happily. Delphine and Alexander roasted one of the acorns. The rich, hot meat warmed them. Hidden inside the tree trunk, they all slept heavily that night, gaining strength for the next leg of the trip. In the morning they turned to the north and followed the river, heading upstream.

The river wound its way deeper into the most forbidding parts of the wintery forest. Even in daytime, it seemed dark. The leafless branches crossed overhead like the bars of Lady Tremaine's mousetraps. At night, the light of the Mimolette moon was barely visible. Cornichonne's winter coat was now so thick that she was able to sleep right on the snow, but Delphine still worried about her. Each night, she created another little glass dome around their campfire to help them keep warm.

Delphine had also started waking in the middle of the night for no reason. Whenever she did, she'd pull out one of the Threaded's illuminated pages and examine it by the glow of her needle, searching for clues.

"Alexander, look," she chirped one morning. He yawned, still tucked between Cornichonne's paws, and rolled over to bury his nose into the cat's fur.

"Look!" she insisted, shaking his shoulder.

He blinked open his bleary eyes.

"I figured something out last night. If I use the illuminated pages as a key, a sort of Mousetta Stone, I can translate each rune in the columns into a letter!"

"So you've been up all night again?"

She wasn't going to let his question derail her. "Not the point." She laid out the pages on her cloak, studying a rune in one illuminated line of text. "This symbol, for example. I think it's the symbol for the letter *T*. Because see where it is on my needle? Seventh symbol from the end? If the last word on my needle is *Twelfth*, then that makes this symbol the *T* in *Twelfth*. Get it?"

Alexander twitched his whiskers, leaning over the pages. "I see—"

"So I can translate the whole alphabet!"

"Does that help us?" asked Alexander, another yawn breaking through. "We don't have anything else to translate."

By this time, their voices had awoken Cornichonne. The cat craned her head around to look at what they were discussing. Delphine heard her snort loudly. She knew what that snort meant.

"Cornichonne, no!" Delphine flung herself over the pages, and not a moment too soon. There was a loud sneeze, and she felt a spray of goo land on the back of her head. She didn't want to think about how much more might be clinging to her cloak, but at least the papers had stayed dry. She could hear Alexander trying not to giggle. "Help me up, please, Alexander," she said with as dignified an air as she could muster.

He eased her up off the papers. She was about to breathe a sigh of relief when she realized that one page had been doused.

"Nutmegs!" She lifted the wet paper by one corner. A large gobbet of Cornichonne goo had hit the page and was oozing downward.

Alexander rushed to her side. "It missed most of the text," he said, trying to be helpful. "Look, that whole area at the bottom, the wettest part, it's blank. Nothing but age stains."

Delphine knew he meant well, but she was so distraught at the potential damage to the page that she couldn't speak. These papers were one of the only links she had to the Threaded. What had she been thinking? She shouldn't have taken them from the pouch, let alone spread them out on the ground.

"I'm sorry," snuffled Cornichonne, her eyes downcast.

Alexander was still staring at the paper as it dangled from Delphine's paw. "Look!" he yelped. "It's not blank anymore!"

She glanced up and gasped. Where the liquid had soaked the paper, pale lines were appearing. Handwriting? Or perhaps even a map?

"A secret message!" cried Alexander. He gamboled around Cornichonne in delight. "Cornichonne, you wonderful, wonderful thing! Look what you did!"

The marks solidified to form a series of hastily scribbled runes. Delphine snatched up the other papers to compare.

"What is that symbol? Alexander, come help me, what is that symbol there?" She shuffled the other eleven pages back and forth, trying to locate each symbol in turn.

"*F . . . I . . . N . . .*" she read out. "*D . . . T . . .*"

"Find!" Alexander crowed. "Find what?"

She ignored him and focused on the symbols. It was painstaking work. "*H*...*E*... 'Find the...'"

Alexander was practically dancing a jig in his excitement. Cornichonne's eyes were perfectly round as she watched.

"No!" Delphine clutched at her whiskers in frustration. "No, no, this symbol doesn't exist!"

Alexander halted in midjig. "Doesn't exist?"

"It's not anywhere in the lines from the rhyme, and those are the only words I know." She ground her teeth.

"Keep on going, Delfie," he urged. "Maybe we can still figure it out."

Letter by letter she translated, until she had *A T E R*, but a dark age stain covered the remaining symbols. "*Ater? Find the ater?* What does *that* mean?" She sat back on her haunches, frustrated.

"No more runes?" asked Cornichonne, peering over Delphine's shoulder.

"That's all I can make out." Delphine pointed to the paper. "This blotch covers the rest."

"*Ater*," Alexander said, rolling the word around in his mouth. "It sounds like a noble's name. Maybe a family name. Lord Ater? Or a title? The Ater of North Peltinore?"

"Who's that?"

He shrugged. "I was just thinking out loud."

"And who says to find *the* Ater? You wouldn't say '*Find the Alexander.*'"

"*You* might not," parried Alexander. "Maybe that's how they spoke back then. After all, we call her the princess. *The* princess."

"But that's her title, it's not—" Delphine felt like she was losing control of the conversation. "Anyway, it looks more like '*Find theater*' than anything else. Maybe there's a theater we need to visit, just how we had to go to a music school."

"But wouldn't you say *the* theater?" Alexander asked.

Cornichonne broke in. "It's a clue, and that's what matters. Let's eat and then we can talk about it as we travel." She licked her lips, and Delphine knew she was thinking about what she might be able to catch for breakfast.

But whether it had gotten too cold for bugs or the cat had poor luck that morning, there was little to be found, and they ventured onward.

For her part, Delphine felt more reassured than she had in a while. It was indeed a clue, and it gave her something to distract her mind from the threat of Midnight. She made a silent promise to her ancestor that as soon as she had taken care of the rats, she would throw all her efforts into following this lead to find *ater* or *theater*, wherever that might be.

Around midmorning, Delphine noticed that Cornichonne's tail was drooping. The lack of breakfast seemed to be getting to the cat. Delphine paused, tugging on Alexander's sleeve to signal him to stop.

"Cornichonne," she said as nonchalantly as she could. "I need to rest my paws for a few minutes. Maybe there are more bugs in this area of the forest. . . . If you want to go on a quick hunt?"

The cat needed no encouragement. She glanced up and down the riverbank to satisfy herself it was safe to leave the two mice, then faded away. Delphine gazed at the tree trunks on the far riverbank. She might as well get in some magic practice while they were waiting.

Needle in paw, she focused on channeling the hatred she felt for the rats into magic, then releasing it in short, sharp blasts. The blue bolts struck tree after tree in quick succession. It was getting easier. She furrowed her brow and threw an extra-powerful bolt from the needle. It sliced through a small tree completely, sending the upper half tumbling to the ground. *If that had been Midnight . . .* She gave a small hiss of success.

Behind her, Alexander cleared his throat.

"Yes?" she snapped, the anger of the blue magic still sizzling in her veins.

His voice was calm and measured. "You're going to kill him, aren't you? That's your new plan."

Delphine stiffened. How did he always manage to know exactly what she was thinking, even when she had no idea at all what was going on in *his* head? "No," she said shortly.

He persisted. "That's why you keep trying to summon more and more of that blue magic, isn't it?"

"Alexander!" she exploded, then felt instantly chagrined. "Look . . ." She struggled to find the words. "He has to be stopped, before he tears apart the kingdom trying to find me. That's why I need to be able to control the blue lightning."

"I'm not sure that stronger magic is the answer. Don't you remember what happened the first night you awoke the needle, on the skiff? It unleashed magic so strong that it nearly killed us."

"The magic was *not* what nearly killed us that night, Alexander. We almost drowned and then were eaten by a pike. *That* was what nearly killed us. Anyway, I'm improving all the time. Yes, it's strong magic, but I can handle it."

Alexander was quiet again. Delphine clenched her paws. He didn't understand. Strength was the *only* way she could defeat Midnight. The strength of hatred. She turned back toward the far riverbank and raised her needle for another round.

"Delfie—" His voice was hard. "This is the wrong path."

She spun on him. "Stop telling me what's right or wrong! You have no idea what you're talking about. I don't need your help, and I don't need *you!*"

He stared back at her. "I'm going to scout ahead," he finally said in a bland voice, barely concealing his hurt.

She watched him head up the shore toward where the river made a sharp turn. Beneath her travel cloak, she was shaking.

She wanted to call him back and apologize, but her mouth refused to open.

She sank onto one of the cold stones that dotted the shore. Just then Cornichonne reappeared, licking her lips. Her tail had perked up.

"Where's Alexander?" she whuffed.

"He's fine." Delphine realized she was reassuring herself as much as Cornichonne. Why in the world hadn't she called out to him to stop? How could she have let him go on alone? Of course, they'd had many disagreements before, but this one felt different. "He went ahead."

Cornichonne wrinkled her nose in concern. She trotted up the riverbank, Delphine behind her.

They had nearly reached the river bend, when she heard Alexander's voice on the other side of the trees. He was talking to someone.

A chill ran down Delphine's tail. She slowed, tiptoeing forward, desperate for a glimpse between the trunks. But the forest was so dense that she couldn't see a thing.

". . . an unexpected pleasure," she heard him saying. "I had thought I was all alone out here."

"Not anymore." This voice was harsh and guttural. It made Delphine's whiskers quiver in terror.

"You report to Midnight, don't you?" said Alexander airily.

There was a short bark of laughter. "How'd ya guess, because we're rats?" came another voice.

Alexander chuckled as if he'd never heard anything funnier in his life. "Because of how strong you all look. Midnight only hires the finest for his ranks."

Delphine felt light-headed. She leaned against Cornichonne's head for support, barely daring to breathe.

Alexander continued, still as cheery as if he were welcoming foreign noblemice to the castle. "I'm awfully glad to finally meet you," he said. "I have information for your leader."

INTERLUDE

R ien paced outside their little alcove, wringing his paws. Elodie was never late. Had something happened? He could feel his heart fluttering in his chest. He tried to take a deep breath.

Just when he was about to break the ultimate rule of the kitchen staff and venture into the upper areas of the fortress, he heard Elodie's quick, delicate steps echoing down the hall. She appeared a moment later, her baby cradled in her arms, her beautiful face lined and tired. Rien hurried to help her sit on one of the old armchairs, and she handed him the child. She began fumbling in her pocket.

"Maturin sent me a letter—"

"He always sends you letters," Rien said, feeling foolish. He wrapped his arms even more tightly around Elodie's baby, as if he could protect her from the terrible world outside their little alcove.

She pulled out a crumpled envelope. "Listen." She unfolded the pages and read out loud, her voice cracking.

My darling—

For days, I have been starting letters to you and then tearing them up. Each time, I think I cannot bear to worry you. But I have decided this cannot wait until my next visit.

I have been warned of a terrible tragedy to come.

Do you recall the badger priest who wedded us? He visited the workshop a few days ago. The abbot of his monastery had come to town, so the priest brought him for a tour of our archives. It should have been a festive occasion, but when the abbot took my paw, his face grew clouded. He told me that a tragedy was about to befall my family—one that would devastate us. He was so earnest, I am afraid to say I believe him.

However, I will not sit by idly waiting for calamity to strike. Already I am building a secret space within the walls of the workshop where we could hide for years, if need be. I will say nothing here about the specific location of these hidden rooms, lest my letter be intercepted. (How can we know whom to trust?)

Perhaps next time I visit, we should all travel back to the workshop together and remain here, close to the secret rooms in case we need to retreat to safety quickly. I know the Threaded have always lived in their castle, but surely you must not die there, too?

Elodie stopped. Rien saw tears sliding down her whiskers, landing on the pages and smearing the ink. Still cradling the baby, he gently took the papers and blotted them dry with his sleeve. His heart ached for her pain, but he could not imagine that the ravings of an old badger abbot were worth putting much stock by.

"You're safe here," he finally said. "The fortress is protected by magic. It's always protected us. Nothing can get in that is unwanted, remember?"

Elodie nodded, sniffling.

"Perhaps it's even safer here than at the workshop," Rien continued, growing more certain as he spoke. "Maybe Maturin should stay here for a time instead. Wouldn't that be allowed?"

"I suppose it would be," said Elodie in a small voice.

Rien nestled the baby back into her arms. She leaned down and kissed the child on the forehead. "I hope he gets here soon," she said, and Rien agreed. Anything to bring the smile back to his best friend's face.

Maturin did indeed arrive a few days later. Elodie told Rien she had persuaded Maturin it would be safest for them all to stay within the fortress grounds. Rien breathed a sigh of relief.

Rien was busy scrubbing out the brick ovens one afternoon when a thin scream pierced the air. He rushed to the windows with the other kitchen staff, but he could not see anything. He ran pell-mell from the room, down the back stairs to the yards. He had never heard Elodie scream, but he was certain that it had been her voice.

From the yards, he could see across the rocks to the edge of the river. It looked as if a body lay there. Mice were pouring from the gates of the castle, running toward it, cradling it. Then the tail of the body twitched.

Rien watched, helpless and terrified. Perhaps he had been wrong. There were so many mice who lived at the fortress. It might not have been Elodie. It must not have been Elodie. The group of mice carried the body back to the fortress and disappeared inside. Fear gnawed at him until he couldn't think.

He tiptoed up the servants' staircase as softly as he could. Thanks to Elodie's descriptions, he had an idea of where her rooms were located. He knew what he was doing was mad, but he didn't care. It would be worth a month of beatings if he could only be certain that Elodie was safe.

He had slipped through a little servants' door into a grand hallway carpeted in rich cobalt, when he heard a babble of mouse voices coming down the corridor. He darted back inside and held the door open a crack. The speakers were headed past him.

"She'll be all right, it's nothing but the shock of it all," came one firm contralto.

"Anyone would be in shock, seeing their husband carried off like that," responded a quavery voice.

"Why didn't she use her magic?" piped up a younger mouse.

"She had no time!" the contralto fumed. "The snake was on them before she ever had a chance. He gave his life to save them."

"Makes me never want to picnic by the river again . . ." said the quavery mouse, and then the voices faded.

Rien stepped back out of the door and onto the cobalt carpet, his heart cold in his chest. They couldn't be talking about Maturin. They couldn't. He peeked around the corner of the next hallway.

He spied a mouse standing guard outside a door, in the process of sending away a nervous little servant. "Leave us," growled the guard. "Elodie's in shock. She has to rest."

Rien made his way slowly back down the staircases, twisting and turning until he had finally reached the lower levels again. He clenched his paws so tightly that he could feel his claws piercing his skin. "She will be fine," he kept saying, because if he kept saying it then it had to be true.

As he reached the kitchens, another terrible thought came into his head. Nobody had said anything about the baby.

That night, it seemed pointless to lie down on the pile of straw that was his bed. Instead, he wandered through the abandoned hallways beneath the fortress. Eventually, he ended up at the little alcove where he and Elodie always met. It was dark inside, but he could hear quiet sobbing.

"Elodie?" he whispered in surprise.

The sobbing stopped. "Hello, Rien," she said, her voice thick with tears. "You can come in."

He stepped inside. It was dark, the moon a new sliver of cheese in the sky, but he could see her shadowy figure curled up on one of the chairs. He lowered himself into the other.

A breathy little whimper came from Elodie's arms, and she lowered her head. "Shush, little one," she soothed.

Relief uncoiled the iron band that had been clamped around Rien's chest. "Is she all right?" he asked before he could stop himself.

"Yes," said Elodie. There was a long silence. "Do you want to hold her?"

Rien had never wanted anything so much in his life. He took the little bundle from Elodie's arms. It was too dark to see the baby's face but he could smell her sweet breath. He sat back down and held her close. He could hear Elodie start to cry again, and wished he could do something for her. Anything.

"Is Maturin—"

She took a deep breath but said nothing.

"I'm sorry," he said hastily.

"No, I . . ." She gulped. "I need to tell you. I want you to know. You loved him, too." Another silence. "Didn't you?"

"I did," he said. He pictured Maturin's jovial face, his boisterous air, how he was beset by hiccups whenever he drank dandelion wine.

"We were picnicking by the river. At the edge of the fortress's grounds. I thought we were still inside the dome of magic, but we must have—" She took a breath to collect herself. "I was napping in the grass when I heard Maturin call out. I'll never forget his voice. As if he already knew it was the last time he would ever say my name. I lifted my head to see a snake with red diamond eyes rearing up over us. Maturin threw himself at it, claws outstretched. He went for its eyes, trying to disarm it, but . . . he didn't make it."

Rien was silent. Even the baby in his arms didn't utter a peep. It was as if the whole world had stopped spinning.

"I was trying to grab my needle, to cast some magic, but it was too late. The snake was already gone." She paused. "It took him with it."

"So you weren't—"

"—hurt? No."

"I saw them picking someone up off the rocks," he said.

"I must have fainted. I couldn't find the strength to go after him." Her voice was heavy. "I'm useless. I couldn't even save my own husband."

"You're not useless," whispered Rien.

The moonlight trickling through the window cast a long, narrow sliver on the floor. A thin silvery line, like the shaft of a needle.

"I'm not?" she said finally.

"Not to me." He reached out in the dark and found her paw. He held it tight.

They sat like that for a long time.

the Ossau-iraty moon

Chapter 15

a squeak of horror escaped Delphine. She clapped her paws over her mouth, praying she hadn't been heard. On the other side of the trees, Alexander chattered away with the rats.

"It's been dismally lonely on my own, chums," he said brightly. "This forest is filled with all manner of odd noises. It's enough to make your tail stand on end!"

She could hear the rats murmuring in agreement. She pictured their beady, unblinking eyes, all staring at Alexander.

"I don't suppose you could point me in the right direction," he continued. "I know Midnight's up this river, but I've got simply the worst memory for directions." He chuckled.

Delphine blinked. What was he playing at?

"As it happens we're going back to Midnight," came the response. Delphine heard the rat sucking on his teeth. "We'll take you there ourselves."

"Brilliant!" Alexander exclaimed. "I think Midnight will be pleased as punch to find out what I have to tell him." But Delphine thought she could hear the quaver in his voice.

"Come on, then," the rat growled. "Don't want you to get lost . . . again." The voice began to fade away.

Delphine felt her legs buckle, and she knew that this time, she *was* going to faint. Cornichonne picked Delphine up in her teeth, holding her as gently as an egg. The cat slunk backward, then turned and raced down the riverbank.

When the cat finally put her down, Delphine collapsed into a puddle of skirts on the icy ground. She buried her face in her paws, her heart breaking. She thought about the last thing she'd said to Alexander: *"I don't need you!"* Nothing could be further from the truth.

Then Delphine felt Cornichonne's raspy tongue licking the top of her head. Oddly enough, it made her feel better. She lifted her head.

"You taste like dirt," said Cornichonne amicably.

"Alexander in the paws of the rats . . . it's all my fault."

The cat considered. "Maybe it's your fault that he went ahead, but I don't think it's your fault that he was captured."

Delphine paused. That was not the response she had expected. "What do you mean?"

"He's a good mouse, so if you hurt his feelings, that was wrong. But he went with those rats on purpose. It must be part of his plan."

Delphine scrubbed her face with her sleeve. "I didn't think of that."

"He'll be all right."

Delphine nodded slowly. "Do you think he knew we were eavesdropping?"

"Yiss." Cornichonne got to work on washing her front paws. "I'm sure of it."

Suddenly Delphine realized exactly what Alexander was doing: getting the rats to lead them straight to Midnight. "All we have to do is follow."

✳ ✳ ✳

They waited until it was dark, knowing Cornichonne would be able to catch up to the rats quickly. Then Delphine settled herself into the saddle on the cat's back, and they tiptoed around the riverbend. There lay rat tracks, as clear as day, and one tiny set of mouse tracks among them, headed due north. Cornichonne moved quietly along their trail.

Before long, the light of a large twigfire came flickering through the trees. They heard carousing up ahead, rat voices raised in song. The coarse tones sent a chill down Delphine's spine.

Without a word, Cornichonne climbed up a nearby tree trunk and crept out onto a thick limb. They peered down into the clearing where the rats had set up camp for the night. Makeshift tents had been cobbled together from cast-off human handkerchiefs. Rats ambled to and fro with supplies.

Delphine didn't see any sign of Alexander. Perhaps he was in one of the tents. Most of the rats were arrayed around the campsite, laughing and singing as they raised mugs in the air.

In the center, several rats danced higgledy-piggledy around the fire. Their tails and ear tips drew dangerously close to the leaping flames as they spun and dipped. Delphine spotted a smaller figure dancing with them. A child rat?

The figure bowed, spun on his paw, and executed a perfect cabriole. Delphine's breath caught in her throat. *Alexander.*

"What is he *doing*?" Delphine cried. But luckily, the rats had chosen that moment to let out a ragged cheer as Alexander gave an elaborate bow, and Delphine's squeaks were drowned out.

She and Cornichonne watched as Alexander drew himself back up, twirling his whiskers with one paw.

"Yer not so bad . . . for a pompous little castle mouse!" One rat guffawed.

Alexander laughed as loudly and gave another fancy bow. "Now, Lonsin, I daresay you think me soft, but I could tell you a tale or two."

Another roar of laughter from the gathered rats. "Go on, then!" growled the rat Lonsin. He passed Alexander a strangely shaped ivory mug sloshing with liquid. Alexander took a sip.

"Well, there I was in the gardens of the castle . . ." began Alexander in his most lordly drawl. "Deep in a game of quoits with the hedgehogs, when what should I see coming up the lawn?" He paused for effect. "Nothing other than a *hawkworm*! Right in the middle of my quoits game! And another, and another! They were all around us! Hawkworms are the most dangerous of all the birdworms, you know."

Delphine covered her mouth with both paws, stifling a laugh. He was trapped in the middle of a battalion of bloodthirsty rats, and what was he doing? Not panicking, not cowering . . . but dancing, drinking, and telling his hawkworm story.

Alexander pranced in front of the fire, demonstrating his prowess as a swordsmouse. ". . . and with one last dashing thrust of my blade, the hawkworms flew straight over the hedges and out toward the ocean, never to be seen again!"

The rats burst into hearty applause, crashing their mugs against one another. "The king'll love that story!" howled the largest one.

Alexander took another sip from his mug. "I'm sure we'll

have many fascinating conversations," he said airily. But Delphine caught a nervous twitch in his tail.

She pulled herself forward until she was up against Cornichonne's ear. "Let's go find a safe place to spend the night," she breathed. The cat nodded silently, already tiptoeing backward along the branch. Back down below, they made their way through the dark trees, letting the sounds of the rats fade away behind them.

Before Delphine had even climbed off Cornichonne's back, she was already gabbling wildly. "I hope he's truly all right. What if he thinks I've abandoned him?"

Cornichonne's face split into that lopsided grin Delphine always found so charming. "What do you think Alexander and I have been talking about whenever you go off to practice your magic? Hawkworms?" Delphine had to laugh. "All he can talk about is how he feels about you. He believes in you more than you believe in yourself. And so do I. We'd do anything to help you, Delphine."

Delphine's laugh caught in her throat. "But don't you see what happens to everyone who's around me?"

Cornichonne gave Delphine a soft snuffle. "I'm still here."

It felt too risky to light a fire or even create a glass dome, with the rats so close. The mouse and the cat crawled inside a hollowed-out fallen tree trunk and curled together into one warm ball of fur. After a little while, Cornichonne began to purr. The rumbling vibrated through Delphine, all the way to the tips of her silvery whiskers.

Only then, as she lay breathing in the smells of old wood and night air, did Delphine remember what Cornichonne had said. *All he can talk about is how he feels about you.* How *did* he feel about her? For that matter, how did she feel about him? The question made her a little hot in the ears. She turned and buried her face in Cornichonne's fur.

✳　✳　✳

Delphine and Cornichonne easily followed the rats' tracks. Each night, they spied on Alexander, checking to make sure he was still hale and hearty. Indeed, he seemed to be thriving in the rats' company, gorging himself on their plentiful rations and dancing around the campfire until the wee hours of the morning.

The winter mists had come down from the mountains. They wreathed through the trees during the days and often lasted until the dark of night. The world around the travelers was a soft gray blur. Days melted one into the next.

Some nights, Delphine practiced with the needle after Cornichonne had fallen asleep. One evening, she returned to find the cat's eyes were open, watching.

"How's it going?" Cornichonne asked in her whuffly voice.

Delphine winced. "I think I'm getting better." She couldn't

tell her friend how much she still struggled to summon true power from the needle.

Cornichonne wrinkled up her nose. "I don't like it when you go away, even to practice. I worry about you."

"Oh, Cornichonne." Delphine rested one paw on the cat's moist nose. "I worry about you, too, coming on this journey with me."

Cornichonne closed her eyes a little. "That's what friends do." She began to purr. "I'm happy to be traveling with you. For most of my life, I always traveled alone. But this is better." The purr grew louder and then became a soft song.

"There once was a mouse both kind and brave,
Who fought for what was right.
In a seaside town she formed a bond
That would keep her safe at night.
This friendship bond was with a cat,
A bond of trust and love.
And so they traveled side by side,
As the moon shone high above."

Delphine tucked herself into the little space below Cornichonne's chin, listening to the cat's quiet song. She was still afraid, but she didn't feel quite so alone.

The next day they began to hear a low hammering. At first it was so subtle that Delphine thought she was hearing her heart beating. Then Cornichonne mentioned it as well, her ears twitching back and forth. The sound grew to a low drumming, ceaseless, tireless, never-ending.

"Is that the rats?" Delphine's voice wavered. The sound set her incisors on edge.

But Cornichonne shook her head. "The tracks keep going," she pointed out. "Whatever it is, the rats are heading toward it."

Ears pressed back against their heads from the strange sound, the two continued east, the thrumming growing ever louder. Suddenly Delphine remembered what the ermine had said about King Midnight's lair—something about the pounding it made in her skull.

The duo came around a bend in the river, and froze. Before them lay a massive stone cliff that towered up to the sky. And tumbling from the top of the cliff was a roaring waterfall. The foamy gray water crashed into the pool below in an endless roll of thunder.

At the top of the waterfall, Delphine noticed a dark, angular shape. She peered through the mist that hung in the air and saw it was a massive fortress, perched atop the craggy rocks. Midnight's fortress. It had to be.

But the area around the base of the waterfall was empty. Where had the rats gone? "Did they climb up the cliffs?" Delphine asked.

The cat looked doubtfully at the sheer rock walls on either

side of the waterfall. "I don't think even I could climb those."

Delphine scampered onto a little hillock nearby. Now she could see a small, dark hole at the base of the cliff, just to the south of the waterfall. And tiny figures were disappearing into it.

She gestured at Cornichonne to join her. "We'll wait until they're all inside."

They watched in silence as the rats filed through the ragged opening in the rock. It reminded Delphine of the gouges on the walls around the Dead City.

Once the last rat had entered, she climbed up onto Cornichonne's back and pulled out her needle, just in case. "Let's go."

At the edge of the pool, Cornichonne let out a flurry of excited mews. Fish were circling within paws' reach in the water; the endless churning of the waterfall was keeping the pool from freezing over. Within seconds, the cat had speared several. Delphine left her to enjoy her well-deserved meal and headed to inspect the hole in the cliff.

"Be careful," said Cornichonne behind her, mouth full.

"I will," promised Delphine. She climbed over the stones that dotted the bank, until she was standing in front of the rough opening. A faint shimmer on the rock face caught her eye. She took a step backward and surveyed the edges. Tiny silver marks were etched on the stone, their delicate shapes contrasted with the rough claw marks. Were those . . . ?

She knelt, examining the ragged chunks of rock on the

ground, left to lie where they had fallen. She turned over one smaller piece, and a silver shape flickered in the pale daylight. She caught her breath.

Threaded runes. Her mind raced. Perhaps, once upon a time, the Threaded had carved runes on the face of this stone wall. And later, as the rats had clawed that opening through the stone, the runes had been destroyed.

But why had the runes been left here in the first place? She gazed up at the opening again, at the few shimmering marks that remained on the wall. There was one place where she could see several runes in a row, if she stood at the right angle. She pulled out the papers to translate.

"Turn away," she spelled out slowly, one symbol at a time. That was all that was left.

Turn away? Delphine shivered. Had this been some sort of warning left by one of the Threaded?

Heart in her throat, she stepped through the opening. She let the needle take on a faint glow. It illuminated a long passageway. The air smelled stale and bitter. She wrinkled her nose, remembering the deepest tunnels in the Forbidden Wing of the castle. This had the same unbearable stench of wet stone and fetid rat droppings.

She tiptoed farther in and found herself at the bottom of a massive pit. A twisting staircase clung to the walls, wending its way upward into the darkness. In the center of the stone floor lay a pile of ancient splintered wood, slowly rotting back into the earth. Claw marks scarred the stone walls. She stared upward, unable to tell how high it stretched.

She trotted back, emerging to find Cornichonne crouching directly outside the opening, her tail twitching. "What's in there?"

"Stairs to Midnight's fortress."

Cornichonne stared at her. "You're going to go up there without me, aren't you?"

"I have to save Alexander. And confront Midnight. This was the plan all along, remember?" Delphine wasn't sure whether she was trying to persuade the cat or herself. The sight of that empty shaft leading up into blackness had sent chills down her tail.

Cornichonne frowned. "The plan never included you heading off on your own into a dark tunnel. You're so tiny. What if you don't come back?"

Delphine felt tears spring to her eyes. "I'll be all right," she insisted. "I'll take supplies." Opening the pockets on the saddle, she withdrew the nearly empty bag of whole nuts and the remaining packets of acorn-flour biscuits she had made in the bats' cave. "And I promise I'll come back for you."

But Cornichonne stared to the north. Delphine followed her gaze and saw how the cliff slowly gave way to steep hills in the distance. "I'm not just going to sit here and wait. I'll head north to those hills. I can climb to the top, then double back south to find you." Tears rolled down the cat's whiskers. "You're my family now."

Delphine rushed forward, throwing her arms around Cornichonne's neck. "You're my family, too," she murmured.

The cat snuffled. "I'll meet you at the top."

Delphine nodded. "But if you can't find me . . ." She gulped. "Go back down and head to the city. Get help." Kissing Cornichonne on her wet nose, Delphine walked through the opening before she lost her nerve.

It was chilly and damp inside, but at least she had left the snow behind. She slipped off her paw covers, blinking away tears and pulling her cloak tight as she moved forward.

Head held high, she began to climb the stairs that would lead her to Midnight, and the fate of the kingdom.

INTERLUDE

In the days after Maturin's death, life in the kitchens grew unbearable. Anytime anyone died upstairs, the kitchen staff always took it upon themselves to be crass and offensive, joking about why the deceased had deserved it. But Rien had never before known any of those who had died. Now he was forced to listen to the other rats around him talking about what an idiot the weaver mouse was to come to the fortress in the first place. Even the mice who worked in the kitchens couldn't spare a kind word for their fellow mouse. They were the worst ones, in fact, calling Maturin a coward for not being able to fight off a snake.

"As if you could," muttered Rien as he washed the flagstones with a wet rag.

"Whazzat?" One of the biggest mice kicked him in the side. "You talking?"

"No." Rien bent back over his rag, scrubbing twice as hard.

But something was building inside him. He had endured their torments for all his life, able to withstand whatever they directed at him. But now to have their cruel words directed at someone he loved, someone who could no longer defend himself, kindled a dark anger he had never felt before.

The breaking point came one night when the kitchen staff began to speak of Elodie.

"Looks like pretty little Elodie ain't married no more," sneered one of the baker rats. "Back on the market, she is."

The biggest and meanest mouse snickered. "You'd make a perfect match. She's even dumber than you." His compatriots nearby burst into laughter.

A red mist rose up before Rien's eyes. He clenched his fists. "Don't talk about her like that."

"No? You gonna defend her?" The mouse let out a coarse laugh. "Nasty little Threaded mouse, thinks she's better than all of us. She shoulda been the one to get eaten up by that red-eyed snake."

"Shut up!" Rien flew at the mouse in a rage. He managed to punch him in the nose once, but then the mouse's companions grabbed him.

"You like fighting?" slurred the mouse, blood dripping from his nose. "You won't like it so much when we're done."

They dragged Rien into a storage room and pummeled him mercilessly. He tried to fight back but there were too many of them, and they took turns beating him. It was as if a dam had broken and all the kitchen staff needed an excuse to take out their anger on someone, anyone.

When he was too broken and battered to care anymore, he closed his eyes and endured the punches and kicks in darkness, waiting hopelessly for death.

Finally, just when he was on the verge of letting go of life, they stopped. It was late, and they were tired. The clicking of their claws on flagstones faded into the distance, along with their laughter. It had been just another ordinary night for them.

Rien was left lying in his own blood. He coughed and warm liquid bubbled from his mouth. He was going to die. He could feel it.

He thought of everything that had happened in his short life. Most of it terrible, but some of it . . . some of it had been wonderful. Elodie and her sweet way of laughing, her nose crinkling. Elodie teaching him to read, even though it had taken years. Her endless patience. Playing games in the hay-loft with smooth river stones. A baby in his arms, pulling on his whiskers.

He didn't have long. He didn't want anything except to see his friend one more time.

With his last ounce of strength, he dragged himself to the back stair-cases. The castle was quiet. It was nearly midnight. He crawled up the steps, climbing higher and higher, away from where he had lived his short life, heading toward Elodie's beautiful world.

He reached the servants' door and crawled out onto the cobalt carpet.

His mouth dripped blood. With eyes nearly swollen shut, he could barely make out the door ahead of him.

He raised one paw and scraped his claws against the wood.

The door swung open. Warm candlelight, the smell of tangerines and roses. Elodie hovered above him, light glowing around her.

"Rien!" she gasped. She dragged him inside, struggling to move his limp body. He could hear her slamming the door and locking it. He gazed up at the ceiling. It was golden and arched, with little fruits painted around the edges. He stared at the apricots and peaches, the grapes and the plums.

Elodie's face leaned over him. "Rien!" she cried. Her tears landed hot on his lips. "Don't leave me!"

He tried to smile, but he couldn't figure out how. He couldn't feel his body anymore.

Her voice sounded so far away. "Rien! I can't lose you, too."

He let his eyes drift closed. His best friend would be the last thing that he saw in this world. That was all he had wanted.

CHAPTER 16

The staircase that led upward had no railing to stop Delphine from plummeting downward if she slipped. She trod as carefully as she could, hugging the walls, even though the steps themselves were wide enough that five mice could easily climb them abreast. The stone of the walls was chilly under her paws and damp from the condensation inside the shaft. Here and there, a shallow alcove room had been carved into the stone, presumably as resting points for weary climbers.

The waterfall caused a deep thrum that vibrated through the stairs beneath her paws, but the booming was muffled and far away. She climbed for hours, noticing little slits carved through the cliff wall where she could look out and see how far up she'd come. She craned her neck for a glance, and mists of the waterfall made the air dreamy outside, like an endless twilight.

Soon she was up high enough that the forest had become a blanket of green flecked with white, stretching out across the land as far as she could see. She was exhausted, and there was no sign of when she might reach the top of the shaft. The air itself was moist and carried the smell of closed-up spaces and ancient stones. Time blurred. The sky outside the slits began to soften with late-afternoon sun.

Just when she was starting to wonder if she would have to sleep in an alcove and continue in the morning, the stairs flattened out. She had finally reached the top. She could see now that the center of the shaft held the remains of a rope and pulley system for moving cargo. It reminded her of the dumbwaiters back at the castle, so long ago. Delphine thought back to the base of the stairs when she had entered, and the pile of wood scraps she had seen there. The rope had rotted away, and the platform had crashed to the bottom.

A passageway led forward into the rock and she followed. It headed upward, leading her to a set of filigreed metal gates that stretched from floor to ceiling. They hung open, covered in cobwebs. She stepped through the gates.

Delphine found herself in a formal hallway like those back at the castle. Thick dust covered every surface. The carpet under her paws was faded, but she could see that it had once been beautiful. She glanced out of the closest window and confirmed her suspicion: she had reached the top of the cliff. She could see that this building sat alongside the river that tumbled down to become the waterfall. *What an odd place to put a building,* she thought, but remembered that this was Midnight's fortress. A perfect place for a lair: inaccessible to all but those allowed to enter.

Delphine crept in silence down the hallways as they branched and turned. All the dusty rooms she passed were decorated in the elegant styles of years long gone by. Marble statues of classic Greek mice lined the hallways, standing between tall windows with long, embroidered curtains pulled back by rich braided ties.

Why would a rat have statues of mice in his fortress? she wondered. Then she began to notice signs of a scuffle. Rat claw marks gouged the wallpaper, and long-dried spatters of blood stained the carpet. She spotted another statue of a Greek mouse, this one lying in marble fragments on the floor. The paintings on the walls showed mice garbed in fashions from hundreds of years earlier, but they all hung dangling in shreds of canvas from their frames, slashed by claws or blades.

A terrible realization washed over Delphine. Midnight hadn't built a fortress at the top of a waterfall. He had invaded a *mouse* fortress and made it his home. She said a silent prayer for the victims and steeled herself. She had to continue on.

She saw more and more indications of a desperate battle, where furniture had been overturned or a door battered in. Beautiful tapestries had been rent in two by vicious swipes of rat claws.

Her needle gave a little shudder in its sheath. She jumped, then remembered how it had led her to the shrine at Fortencio Academie, where the ghost of Cecile had appeared and shared a vision of her ancestor. Was the needle trying to lead her somewhere again? She pulled it out and let it rest in her paw like a compass needle. When she took a step forward, the needle tingled.

The hallway split and the needle guided her left, then up a broad flight of stairs. These rooms were even more grand. Damask courting sofas and cherrywood side tables stood silent and abandoned. This had to be the central part of the fortress, she thought. But where was Midnight?

She stepped paw into one of the grand rooms just as the sun broke through the clouds at the horizon. Late-afternoon light cascaded in through the windows. Her breath caught in her throat. She could now see that a row of carved runes ran all the way around the top of the room.

She dashed down the hall, looking at everything in a new light. The runes were there in every room, some painted, some carved, all repeated over and over. How could she have not noticed them? She turned a corner and saw a huge painting ahead, facing a set of massive double doors. This had clearly once been the main entrance to the fortress. The painting featured Rhapso and Arachne, the mice of Threaded legend, and the frame was so large that it seemed as if the two mice were standing in the hallway with her.

In the painting, moonlight poured down around the two mice, pooling in Rhapso's paws, where she manipulated a spindle. She was spinning the moonlight into a fine silver thread, Delphine realized. The thread ran from the spindle to Arachne's paws. Elaborate gold-and-silver runes shimmered around the edges of the painting.

Fingers trembling, Delphine pulled out the old pages from her bag to translate the runes.

"*Turn away . . .*" began the phrase. Her paws shook. Those were the same words she had seen at the bottom of the stone cliff, carved over the entrance to the stairs. But why would this warning be written on a painting of Rhapso and Arachne? She kept translating.

"*. . . from fear, and turn toward light. Turn away from fear, and turn toward light.*" The phrase was repeated over and over, all the way around the painting in a silvery halo that encircled the two mice. It was a maxim. Words to live by. It wasn't a warning at all.

Had that been the message carved into the stone at the base

of the waterfall as well? A way to keep travelers' spirits strong? But why would the Threaded have placed this message in and around a random mouse fortress on a waterfall?

The waterfall . . . her breath caught in her throat. The papers had said *Find the ater* in Threaded runes. It hadn't been a name like Ater, and it hadn't been *theater,* either. It had been a word, with most of its letters hidden beneath the stains of age. *Find the waterfall.* Someone long ago had left that clue, and she had completely missed it.

Delphine reeled in realization at what she was seeing. The runes carved and painted everywhere. The elaborate tapestries, hanging torn on the walls. The gates she had entered, covered in silvery swirls like the magic of the needle. The building itself, perched atop the rocks with mist billowing around it. Mist that billowed like *clouds.* She had been blind to not see it sooner.

Delphine was standing inside the castle in the clouds—the castle of the Threaded.

✳ ✳ ✳

When she was finally able to calm herself, she tried to think. This had once been the Threaded's home. There was no doubt in her mind.

Why in the world had the rats led her here? Understanding stabbed through her with a sharp, icy pain. King Midnight hadn't claimed just any fortress as his own. He had claimed *their* fortress—the Threaded's. It was he who had taken them from this world, right here.

She smoothed back her whiskers and took a deep breath. She had come this far. It was time to complete her quest. She continued along the wide hallways, letting the needle lead her with its vibrations. She saw fresh pawprints in the dust, heading in the same direction that the needle was telling her to go. A rank, foul odor was growing in the air.

She turned a corner and gagged as she was hit with the smell of rotting meat and wet, filthy fur. She heard coarse voices coming from a doorway farther down the corridor. She tiptoed toward it, her heart pounding. The stench was now so bad that she could taste it. Her needle trembled madly in her paw. It was leading her to whatever was in that room.

Delphine swallowed hard, now right outside the open door. She pressed herself up against the wall, biting her lip. Was she strong enough to do this? She hadn't been able to fully master the blue lightning. But now she was out of time, and she had no choice. Gripping her needle, she summoned the magic of hatred until it was crackling beneath her paws.

She could hear the voices laughing and snarling. She took one last breath and stepped inside.

KING MIDNIGHT SAT ON HIS THRONE, trying to act as if nothing was the matter. His scars throbbed like lines of fire eating away at his body. After more than a hundred years of immortality, his body was falling apart, and it had all begun on that night, some months ago, that the last needle had been found.

And so, just this morning, he had made the decision. He could wait no longer. He would call for everyone in his service to gather before him at dusk, and then he would send them *all* out after that mouse— every one of his troops, every one of his guards. He shivered at the thought that he would soon be alone in his fortress with nobody but the dead for company, but the time for prudence had passed.

As the sun fell toward the horizon, his minions assembled in his throne room, drawn by his command. Mezzo barked orders, herding everyone into neat rows, but Midnight barely noticed. In the last few hours, the pain had escalated into unbearable agony. His scars felt as if they were melting into his skin. After all these years, was he finally going mad?

Through the open doors of his throne room, a tiny figure charged into the fray. It was a mouse, here in the heart of his hidden fortress. Her whiskers shone silver in the firelight. And in her paw, she held a shining silver needle.

Chapter 17

Delphine had run straight into the heart of the rats' lair. Guards swarmed, their beady eyes gleaming. Behind her, she could hear more rats moving to block the doorway. She glanced around, desperate to figure out why the needle had brought her to this place. She could see it once had been an elegant drawing room, but now was little more than a stage for filth.

There was no sign of Alexander. Her heart fell.

Then she noticed the dark figure that sat on the throne at the center of the room, outlined by the last rays of daylight streaming through the windows behind him. Though she had never seen him before, she knew him in an instant.

King Midnight laughed, his fangs long and yellow. "Welcome, little mouse," he said. His voice curled around Delphine like an oily eel. "Thank you for bringing the needle back to me. I've been waiting for more than a century for this moment."

Rage coursed through Delphine's body and into the needle in her paw. It sparked with vicious blue fire, and King Midnight's eyes widened. But before she could point the needle at him, the rat guards grabbed her. She pivoted to blast the closest guard and he flew backward with a yelp. More rats were closing in. She fired desperate bolts of blue lightning, but there were too many of them. They shoved her to the ground and stomped on her paw holding the needle, pressing her knuckles down against the stones. She lay gasping, the breath knocked out of her.

King Midnight rose slowly from his throne. Behind him, a rat guard with a white blaze on her face stood tall and silent. She watched with implacable finality, as if Delphine were a lowly insect or a useless object to be discarded. Midnight knelt and plucked the needle from Delphine's paw, a hungry glow in his eyes.

"No!" Delphine strained against the rats' grips.

King Midnight's lips peeled back from his fangs in a twisted grin. He turned toward the mantelpiece of the drawing room's main fireplace. Only then did Delphine see what was arranged along it.

Eleven mouse skulls.

They were old, fragile bones crumbling. She cried out. The rage bubbled up even hotter inside her, and she bit down on one of the paws that was holding her.

The rat howled and hissed, and smashed her alongside the head with his fist. Still, she kept biting and kicking with all her strength. Somehow, she managed to wriggle away. She dashed toward Midnight, but before she could reach him, another guard grabbed her tail and yanked her backward. She scrabbled to pry the paws off her, but it was no use. The rat had her in a viselike grip.

King Midnight moved toward the mantel, the needle resting solemnly in his paws. "At last," he crowed. "At last!"

Delphine followed his gaze upward.

Above each skull hung a needle of the Threaded, exactly like her own. Eleven of them. Her eyes widened. Those were the skulls of the Threaded.

Eleven skulls. Eleven needles.

And she had the twelfth.

Delphine's head was spinning. Then she had been right. Her ancestor had been the only Threaded to escape Midnight's fury.

King Midnight raised the needle with a wordless yowl of victory that chilled her. Again, she twisted against the rats' paws.

The rat with the blaze watched, her eyes still devoid of emotion.

King Midnight slowly turned and looked at Delphine, as if truly seeing her for the first time. Delphine froze. "Take her away until I decide what to do with her," he ordered with a flick of his wrist.

The guards began to drag her toward the door. "Where's Alexander?" she cried. "What have you done to him?"

Ignoring her, King Midnight turned once again toward the mantelpiece. He leaned forward and placed her needle below the others that hung on the wall.

That's why the needle began to tingle, she realized. *It sensed the presence of the other eleven.*

The rats shoved her through one corridor, then another, until she lost track of how far they'd gone. They arrived at a crumbling tower, where they threw her into a small circular room. She could hear them locking the door and posting a guard outside.

"Alexander?" she called, hoping he might be in an adjoining cell. She called out again and was rewarded by the slam of a rat's fist on the door.

"Silence!" the guard bellowed.

She peered out of the narrow windows of her tower cell, and her heart sank. It was a long, sheer drop to the rocks below. Through the dark, she could just see the edge of the river as it rushed toward the cliff to throw itself off into thin air. A strange glowing web of lines hung in the air around the fortress. Some sort of magical protection, left over from long ago?

Fighting against the terror that threatened to overwhelm her, she took a deep breath. It wasn't over yet, she reminded herself. She looked around. She was no longer in the luxurious part of the castle. The tower room was bare, with uneven wooden floors and whitewashed walls. A heap of junk had been shoved into one corner: a wobbly stool, a poorly mended broom, wads of thistledown. A massive pile of long, rectangular rugs lay nearby—no, not rugs—small tapestries. By the look of the torn loops across the tops, Delphine could guess they had been ripped down by the rats from the wall where they had once hung.

Curious, Delphine sat on the stool and began to examine the tapestries.

They were so fragile that she could only lift one at a time. She realized quickly that they were all portraits of Threaded mice, each holding a needle. There were so many of them, far more than twelve. She was looking at generations of Threaded stretching back through time. Clouds of dust rose from the ancient fabric as she moved them. She sneezed nearly as loudly as Cornichonne. She realized quickly that each tapestry was a portrait of a Threaded mouse, holding a needle. She had blown away most of the dust, and the mouse's whiskers were now shimmering. She rubbed a careful paw across them, revealing silver thread that gleamed in the thin light. She flipped gently through the top of the stack, brushing the worst of the dust away as she went. Every one of the Threaded had been embellished with whiskers of silver thread.

She studied the top tapestries carefully, turning them this way and that, looking for hidden runes or any other clues that could help her. It was to no avail.

Deciding she'd gotten the most she could out of the tapestries, Delphine restacked them, then circled the room again, examining each crack and crevice for weaknesses. But there were none. Without her needle, there was no way to escape. She would have to wait until the guards came back for her in the morning.

The events of the day overtook Delphine. She was exhausted. She pushed all the thistledown into the corner farthest from the windows, hoping to avoid the worst of the cold night air, and curled up in it. She had thought it would be hard to relax enough to sleep, but as soon as her eyes drooped shut, she was gone.

Delphine dreamt yet again of the thread leading her through twisting hallways, its silver hue now dimmed to a deep, shadowy shade of gray. She passed through a set of gates and followed the dark thread until she found herself back in the tower room of Midnight's fortress, where she had fallen asleep. In the darkness, the pile of tapestries glowed silver. She heard a voice: *"Find the knot . . ."*

A massive clanging tore her from her uneasy slumber. It was the bell of a clock tower, counting out the hour. There had been no ringing of the bell for any previous hour of the day or night, but now it tolled and tolled. In the dark, she counted twelve. Then all fell silent again.

$$* \quad * \quad *$$

Delphine awoke to a thin winter light creeping through the window. She crawled out of the dusty mound of thistledown. Now that it was day, she could truly see the area around the fortress for the first time. It stood perched at the top of the waterfall, on a ledge of rocks and stones. Flat gray sky stretched to the horizon. There was no sign of Cornichonne. She looked upward. In the daylight, the gleaming web of lines that arced over the fortress was less noticeable.

The guards would be here any minute. She did her best to comb through her whiskers and brush the worst of the dust from her ears and face. Then she carried the stool to the center of the room and sat facing the door, waiting.

The daylight slowly crawled across the floor. Delphine grew thirsty, then hungry. Finally, she banged on the door.

"Hello?" she called. Had they forgotten about her? Had she been left to die? Panic welled up inside her. "Hello!" she cried out. "Help me!"

Silence. She wiped angry tears from her eyes and tried to distract herself by going back to the window again.

A key rattled in the door, and she whirled around. It was one of Midnight's rat guards, tall and lean, with a rangy look and a white blaze on her face.

"Stay there, mouse," she ordered. She placed an ivory mug of water and a plate of dry acorn crumbs on the floor. The mug looked like those Delphine had seen the rats using in camp. "I heard the morning shift hadn't bothered to bring your rations."

Delphine blinked. "Thank you," she finally forced herself to say. It made her blood run hot to have to speak to a rat, let alone *thank* one, but she would not forsake her manners.

"Leaving a prisoner without food or water." The rat curled her lip in disgust. "They're monsters."

Now Delphine knew where she had seen this rat before. She had been in the throne room with Midnight the night before. Delphine noticed a ragged notch in one ear. Had that happened during a battle with mice? Anger rose up in Delphine.

"You're *all* monsters!" she snarled. "You care about nothing except yourselves, and how many innocent lives you can take."

The rat's expression darkened, but she said nothing.

"Monster," growled Delphine again. She knew the rat could kill her with a single slash of her powerful claws, but she was beyond caring. She would not be silent.

"My name is Mezzo," the rat said in a low thunder. "But call me Monster if you wish. It makes no difference to me."

She closed the door and Delphine heard the bolt shoot home in the lock.

The acorn crumbs were stale, but Delphine wolfed them down. When she picked up the ivory mug, she realized why it was so oddly shaped: it was fashioned from the skull of a newt, lined with fired clay. She nearly dropped it, repelled, but her thirst overtook her. Saying a silent prayer for the newt, she gulped down the foul water.

The day wore on. She sat, then stood, then paced, then sat again. Midafternoon, desperate for any distraction, she turned her attention to the pile of tapestries that had glowed in her dream. She began to clean them one by one, gently wiping off the dust and dirt. She polished the metallic threads of their whiskers with a corner of her travel cloak. And, little by little, the silver thread started to take on a faint glimmer. It wasn't just the whiskers that were glimmering, she realized: once cleaned of dust, the tapestries shimmered with a faint light.

Each of the tapestries featured a name across the bottom in swirling letters. *Ertice, Maydeline, Claudien*—she recognized some of them from the names on the tapestries at Château Trois Arbres.

As she made her way slowly down through the pile, meticulously cleaning the dust from each, she realized that the garments of the Threaded in the tapestries were becoming more modern. The ones on top had been wearing medieval garb, but now these other outfits were only a few hundred years old. If they had been hung in order, they would have been pulled down in that same order, she reasoned. And if so, the last twelve at the bottom would be the most recent twelve of the Threaded.

A thought struck her. One of these final portraits had to be of her ancestor. Delphine would finally be able to see what she had looked like. A lump formed in her throat.

Dusk fell as she cleaned the final twelve with particular care, polishing the whiskers on each one to a gleam. When she reached the last portrait, the name at the bottom of the portrait leapt out at her.

ELODIE.

The same mouse who had written the letters she'd found! Elodie gazed outward, her green eyes full of compassion, but the tapestry lacked the same magical shimmer as the rest. The portrait was dull and lifeless.

Delphine's heart sank. Then she noticed a loose bit of thread at the lower edge of the tapestry: a few rows remained undone. Delphine felt compelled to finish the work. It only took a moment for her to fashion a makeshift needle from a straw of the discarded broom, but the little hanging strand of thread was too short to complete the job.

Wait! Suddenly she remembered the thread fragment she had found in the Threaded's private room in the Dead City. She dug through her pocket, finally finding it half-stuck in the seam. It was a different color, but it would do. She knotted the little piece onto the end of the hanging strand and began to weave it through the tapestry.

With the scrap of silver thread, she finished the last few stitches. Night had fallen and the little tower room had grown dark. She tied off the thread and snipped it neatly with her incisors, then spread the tapestry on the floor and stepped back to see the full effect.

The portrait now shimmered with the same gentle light as all the others. Delphine smiled, proud of herself. Elodie's green eyes seemed practically to be glowing.

Delphine looked again. They *were* glowing. The shimmering around Elodie's figure was growing stronger by the second. The portrait felt alive. Delphine could almost believe that the mouse in the portrait could see her. And she looked so familiar, as if Delphine had always carried this face deep within her heart. Those green eyes . . . so much like her own.

She remembered how she had called to Cecile in the abandoned tunnels of Fortencio Academie.

"Elodie?" she whispered to the tapestry. "Who were you?"

The silver light of the tapestry flickered like flames, casting sparks of light around the tiny room.

Delphine rubbed her eyes. The tapestry slowly floated off the ground, the shimmer now so bright that she could barely look at it.

"*Delphine . . .*" The light started to wrap around her like a warm hug.

The gentle voice came again, more strongly. ". . . I am here with you." A figure was emerging from the tapestry, points of silvery light like stars coming together to form a solid being.

And then Elodie stood before her, her silver whiskers glowing, more solid than a ghost. She reached out one paw, and Delphine slowly reached back. Their paws touched. This mouse was real.

Elodie's amber fur blended into rings of white around her eyes and ears, but it was her radiant smile that made her truly lovely.

"Delphine," she said softly, gazing across a hundred years.

Delphine opened her mouth, but nothing came out.

"My brave Delphine," the shimmering mouse said. "I've waited for so long to tell you the truth. Now I finally can."

Delphine was transfixed. "What truth? Are you my ancestor?"

The stars that made up Elodie's body all seemed to sparkle in unison, and her whiskers glimmered in the light. She let out a faint laugh. "I suppose you could say that. I'm your mother."

Chapter 18

Delphine felt the room spin around her. Impossible. Elodie had been dead a hundred years before Delphine was born.

And yet, she thought, *that would explain why the magic of the Threaded is so strong inside me. It wasn't diluted across generations.*

"My mother?" she whispered.

"Yes," Elodie replied. She touched Delphine's cheek, her soft paw like chiffon whispering against Delphine's fur.

Delphine shook her head, wanting desperately to believe but

not understanding. "How can that be?" It was her *mother* who had fled from the rats? Her mother who had sought shelter at the music school, then the monastery? That meant the baby . . .

Delphine gasped.

"Let me tell you how I came to leave you on that doorstep," Elodie said. "I only hope you can forgive me for what I had to do. And I hope you will be able to right the wrongs that were left undone when I died."

So her birth mother was truly gone. Delphine knew it had to be so, if she had lived a century ago, but it still tore her heart apart to hear those words. Hot tears rolled down her cheeks.

"I have been dead for a century, my sweet. Listen and I shall start at the beginning.

"We lived in this fortress." Elodie gestured at the walls around her. "We called it the Castle of the Threaded. And the twelve of us, we were the current Threaded. Born of the Threaded bloodline, we were destined to carry on the work that had begun long before us. There had always been twelve Threaded, and there would always be twelve—no more, no less—creating happiness and light, in the smallest and largest of ways. We could make flowers bloom in midwinter and bring rainbows down to touch the land.

"But there were some magics that were forbidden. We were not allowed to bring back the dying, for to interfere with life and death would be to alter the thread of fate. And we were forbidden from meddling with the thread of Time, because the past cannot be changed, and we could not know how we might alter the future."

"I found Threaded documents in one of the Dead Cities," remembered Delphine. "They listed those same warnings."

Elodie nodded. "We were fortunate to live such a privileged life, although I was lonely. I was by far the youngest. The others were practically adults already, so I had no friends . . . until I met a little rat named Rien, who swept the hearths in the kitchen. We became fast friends, as close as a sister and brother.

"As we grew, we confided more and more in each other. When I first fell in love with your father, Maturin, I whispered to Rien about the dashing mouse I had met."

Delphine pictured the stack of envelopes from the workshop. "I read the letters you wrote to him!"

"Then you know we met during one of the Threaded's trips to the tapestry workshop of Montrenasse-sur-Terre. He was the most handsome mouse I had ever seen. And when he proposed, Rien was the first to hear the good news. He was so happy for me." Elodie sighed. "Rien had such a huge heart. But nobody else could see it. The other rats and mice who worked in the kitchen bullied and teased him mercilessly. Maturin grew close to Rien as well, and would ask him to keep me company whenever he traveled back to the tapestry workshop. He was gone for weeks, sometimes, but that just made our time together that much sweeter. And soon we had a new baby."

Delphine looked around the tower room, imagining what

life had been like here at the Castle of the Threaded, a hundred years ago. Elodie rocking their baby in the cradle as Maturin sat nearby. Perhaps they had snuggled up in front of a cozy fireplace.

"But then I lost Maturin." Elodie's beautiful eyes filled with tears. "He died protecting us. My world broke in two that day. I was inconsolable. Even sweet honeycomb turned bitter in my mouth. I let myself become lost in the depths of my grief.

"Rien tried to comfort me as best he could. Then came the day when he stood up to the kitchen bullies—defending Maturin's honor, from what I gathered. They beat him savagely. He lay dying at my door, my best friend, all because he had had the courage to defend my husband's good name. It was too much to bear."

Despite Delphine's ingrained fear of rats, she found herself feeling pity for Rien as Elodie told her tale. "The other rats? Why would they do that?"

Elodie's voice was low. "Because they could." She paused, and her face twisted. "But it wasn't only the rats. There were mice who worked in the kitchen who bullied him as well."

A rat . . . bullied by mice? Delphine struggled to understand. "I thought we mice were the good ones . . ." She trailed off, feeling confused.

There was a terrible, deep sadness around Elodie. "Most mice are good. A few are not. It's true not only for mice, but for rats, for shrews, for newts, for every creature in this kingdom."

"Even cats." Delphine gulped, remembering the assumptions she had made about Cornichonne when they had first met. "So there are truly good rats?"

Elodie shrugged. "My best friend was one. I have to believe there are more."

The silence hung between them until Delphine could bear it no longer. "Did he die?" she asked in a small voice.

"Yes and no." Elodie twisted her paws together, a nervous gesture so familiar to Delphine that it was as if she were watching herself in a mirror. "I tried to stanch his wounds, but the blood was coming too quickly. His eyes were filmy."

Delphine's stomach clenched as she remembered Louis as he had lain dying by the refugees' campfire.

"His body was so starved and stunted that he had no strength left to hang on to life. But I had just lost Maturin, my true love. Losing my best friend as well . . . I couldn't bear the thought."

Her voice fell until it was little more than a whisper. "I knew that the magic of the needle must never be used to cheat death, but I was past caring. I grabbed it from its rosewood case and let my fear flow through me into the forbidden magic. With the silver thread we reserved for only our most powerful spells, I sewed up his wounds. Slowly, the blood ceased to flow, and his skin began to knit back together, stitch by stitch."

Delphine imagined Elodie bent over Rien's poor, beaten body, silver thread in paw. Was that why the shred of thread she had used to repair Elodie's tapestry had summoned her? Was the shining thread really that powerful?

"My poor Rien was still so weak. I put him in my bed and slept on the sofa, nursing him back to health. But something terrible was happening to him. I didn't want to admit it, but I could see why we had been warned to never cheat death. Whatever was in his mind at the moment of my spell, that was who he would be forever more. In short, he was no longer my Rien."

"Who was he?" whispered Delphine.

"A creature made of anger—at his attackers, at the injustice of it all. It overwhelmed the good inside him." Elodie's voice caught, and she pressed one paw to her eyes. "The more he healed, the more his hatred consumed him, powered by the needle's magic. It spread to his heart, where it tarnished the silver thread, turning it dark."

"The needle had only been able to save the parts of him that hadn't yet died," said Delphine, finally understanding.

"When at long last he mustered the strength to rise from the bed, I could see his body itself had grown, as if his hatred needed more space than his once-small frame could hold. Every day, as he continued to heal in my chambers, his strength grew, and so did his thirst for revenge.

"Still I hoped I could lead him back to being the sweet, gentle rat he had been before. Was I naive? Perhaps, but I believed goodness persisted within that spiderweb of scars and hate."

The look on Elodie's face told Delphine that the worst was

yet to come. "Then one day, I returned to my quarters to find that in a fit of rage, he had shattered all the windows. He stood at the center of the room, glass clutched in his paws.

"His voice was hoarse. 'The mice, they're evil. I see it now. No other rat shall ever be beaten and threatened and tormented as I have. It is time to have my revenge.' His eyes were wild."

Suddenly Delphine didn't want to hear any more. She didn't want to know how the walls of the fortress had become splattered with blood.

But Elodie continued. "I was overcome with horror at what I had unwittingly helped to create. 'I've always loved you, and I'm a mouse,' I begged him. 'Am I so terrible?'

"He gripped my paws. 'Not you. But you have no idea how I've suffered. The mice must fall. The rats must rise. And you must come with me. I will keep you safe. Elodie, don't abandon me now.'

"I was sobbing. 'You're no longer the Rien I knew,' I cried. 'You've become a monster.' I ran to the cradle for my little one. I had unleashed a great evil within the fortress of the Threaded, and I didn't know how to stop it."

"But how could he turn on you like that?"

A tear slid down Elodie's cheek. "That was my question as well. 'This doesn't have to be,' I said. 'We can remain family as we were before.' He stood silent, and for one moment, I dared to hope. But then he raised his fists, smashing them against the stone walls so hard that the floor shook.

"I screamed and threw open the door, running blindly. I could hear him cursing and howling. I had no idea where I was going, only that I had to save my darling baby—*you*."

Delphine's mind was racing. She remembered how she had felt when she had gazed upon the centuries-old Dead City, as if she were looking at home. A hundred years ago *was* home to her, once upon a time.

Elodie's whiskers shimmered in the moonlight. "I ran through the fortress. I could already hear mice screaming in the distance, and the snarls of angry rats. We Threaded weren't warriors. The location of our home was our protection. Perched at the top of a cliff, surrounded by a net of magic, it was impregnable from any outside attacks. But this attack was coming from the inside.

"I could hear the rats getting closer. They were laughing, egging one another on. One cried out, 'Remember what Rien told us, our time has come!' I heard the bell in the fortress tower begin to chime out the hour. It echoed in the night air, twelve resounding booms. The rats were cheering. 'Midnight! Our rebellion begins at the stroke of midnight!' They were everywhere. It was too late to do anything but flee, as far and as fast as I could."

"Midnight," Delphine whispered.

"I fled, and he sent his rats after me. He wanted my needle . . . and he wanted *me*. They pursued me halfway across the kingdom. I hoped at first that I could find somewhere safe to hide. Maturin had told me he had built secret rooms inside the walls of his tapestry workshop, but he had not had time to show me where before he died, and I knew the workshop would be the first place the rats would look. So I headed west, and south. I lied to cover my tracks, saying I was a nobody who had stolen a needle from the rats. I couldn't risk anybody discovering I was one of the Threaded. But wherever I went—a farm, a monastery—I could never lose the rats for long. They had my scent, and they would never stop. Loose fragments of an idea began to form. There was only one way left to save your life, and I would do it, no matter the cost.

"One night, the rats were so close, I could hear their snarls echoing behind me. I hobbled through the woods, hoping to find a place to carry out my ultimate plan. I was in luck. I stumbled upon a human château in good condition, with a well-kept mouse entrance.

"I laid you on the mouse doorstep, still swaddled in linens from the monastery. You let out a frightened squeak in the cold night air, and my heart broke in two. I had to remind myself that if this worked, you would be safe. With enough time, the rats would give up their hunt for the mouse with the needle and a baby, and when you finally reappeared, you would be nothing more than an orphan left on a doorstep. Nobody would think to connect you with the mouse who had disappeared long ago.

"With my needle, I wove forbidden magic around you, lifting you out of time altogether. I felt in my bones I could do it, and I was willing to risk the consequences. I fed as much magic into the spell as I could, hoping to make it strong enough to last for many years."

Delphine's heart pounded. So she had been right. It *had* been her birth mother who had left her on that doorstep.

"Only when the spell was drained of magic would you pop back into time. The Threaded would be gone. The needle would be nothing more than a curiosity, but at least it would connect you to your past. . . ."

"But without the needle, how could you protect yourself?" interrupted Delphine.

Elodie smiled sadly. "It was safer than letting the rats get their paws on it."

Her sacrifice pierced Delphine's heart.

"I watched as the bundle vanished in a shower of silver sparks. It was time for the second half of my plan—to draw the rats away from the doorstep. I waited until they began to appear, and then I darted into the woods. It was only a matter of time before they caught me, but I wouldn't make it easy for them. I fought to the end."

Chapter 19

*e*lodie's voice grew quiet, her eyes sad. The moonlight sparkled on her figure as she floated in the tiny room.

Delphine sniffled, then rubbed at her face. "It worked," she
said. "The needle kept the spell charged for a hundred years."

Elodie smiled. "Now you can finish what I started. You
must confront the monster that Rien has become, and right
the wrong. Undo the spell I should never have cast. The silver

thread that holds his heart together has grown dark. Find the first stitch of the thread and unravel the magic. Only that can end the war between rats and mice." Elodie began to shimmer, turning into a cloud of silvery stars before Delphine.

"Wait!" Delphine gasped, struggling to keep her voice down. "How do I find the thread?"

The stars were already disappearing back into the fibers of the tapestry.

Delphine was desperate now. "Elodie! M-Mother!"

But the last of the silvery sparks were gone.

The tapestry lay again on the ground, as silent and still as all the others. Only the faintest glimmer remained.

Delphine curled into a ball, rocking herself, sobbing until she thought her heart would break. When she could cry no more, she lay quiet, thinking, going over and over all that Elodie had told her.

Midnight—*Rien*—was the one who had lit an evil fire in the rats to wreak revenge against all mice. It was his words that had spread like a cancer across the kingdom, poisoning every rat they touched. He had been living—no, not living, *existing*—in this fortress for more than a hundred years, biding his time, trying to harness the power of the needles.

She paced back and forth in her cell, turning over the words of her birth mother. Undo the spell. Undo the spell that had saved Rien's life, Elodie must have meant. But she couldn't see how.

Find the first stitch, Elodie had said. It made her think of what Maman had said so long ago: *You just need one place to start. Find the knot.* All Delphine had to do was find the starting place, the dark thread, and she could unravel the spell.

The ominous tolling of the bell began, as it had the night before. Once again, she counted to twelve. It was midnight. She laughed at the absurdity. Did Midnight force his minions to ring the bell every night?

Clamoring voices and banging in the hallway interrupted her thoughts. The guards were coming. She took a deep breath and stood tall.

The key clattered in the lock, and the door was thrown open. It was the same guard as the day before. Mezzo.

"Mouse, come with me." She stepped forward, moving toward Delphine.

Delphine pulled her cloak even tighter and headed toward the door. She wasn't going to give any rat the excuse to lay paws on her.

In the hall, three more guards waited. Mezzo led the way while the rest fell in behind Delphine. They started up a tightly winding set of stairs. The stone steps were worn low in the middle from centuries of paws traveling up and down. The guards behind her forced her upward with the tips of their spears.

Delphine wondered if her birth mother had ever come up these stairs. She remembered Alexander on the first day she had met him back at the castle, pointing out the door that led up to the clock tower. How he had spoken of taking her to visit it one day.

I'm coming for you, Alexander, she thought. *As soon as I take care of what needs to be done.*

The door at the top of the stairs was already ajar, a sliver of night sky peeking in. The rat behind pushed her through, and she found herself standing on the roof of the fortress's tallest tower. They were up so high that the river below was nothing but a silvery smudge wending its way toward the edge of the cliff.

The black sky overhead was pocked with points of light. Were those the stars? No. She realized she was seeing the same glowing net of protection she had seen from her window the night before. Now that she was outside looking up, she could see how it enclosed the fortress on all sides. Glimmering lines drew arcs across the sky, creating tiny dots of white light whenever they intersected. It was as if the Threaded had once harnessed the stars of the night sky to watch over them. *It's remained even with all the Threaded gone,* she thought.

The rat guard pushed her forward, and she stumbled farther onto the rooftop. A row of rats stood across from her. Most had bows and quivers of arrows on their backs. She was beginning to understand how Midnight had been able to rain down terror on the kingdom during the War to End All Wars.

The peaceable farmers and townspeople had never stood a chance.

Sharp wind cut across the roof and Delphine shivered, her ears numb in the freezing air. Behind her, claws grated on stone. She spun around. There loomed Midnight, his face crisscrossed with cruel scars.

He laughed. "Little one! You've come to tell me the secret of the needles."

Delphine held her head high, trying not to show her fear. "Your guards forced me here."

One corner of his mouth cocked upward. "Defiance won't get you far with me. I've lived too long." He surveyed her for a moment, his face flat again. "Tell me how to use the needle."

"I'm not telling you anything." She was desperate to know where her needle *was*, but she refused to give him the satisfaction of showing that she cared.

"I had a feeling you would say that." His voice was lazy, curling around her like a hungry snake. "So I've brought someone who might be able to talk some sense into you."

"I don't think so."

Midnight's lips peeled back in earnest this time, a terrible smile splitting apart his face. "Oh, but *I* do." A small figure stepped out from behind him.

Alexander.

Delphine caught her breath. He didn't appear as if he'd been in a dungeon. In fact, his garments all looked freshly brushed and pressed.

He winked at her with a jaunty tilt of the head. "My lady," he called out nonchalantly.

Midnight's voice grew even quieter. "Don't you want to hear what he has to say?"

Delphine ignored Midnight's taunts. She was staring at Alexander, trying to see what was in his eyes. He looked . . . pleased?

"My lady!" Alexander called out again, with even more enthusiasm. "You really must make a proper acquaintance of our host. Did you know that he styles himself as a king?"

Midnight whirled on him, eyes blazing. "You're on thin ice, little mouse."

Alexander laughed jauntily, and a shiver of fear ran down Delphine's spine. Wasn't he afraid?

Alexander grinned even more broadly than before. "As thin as the ice on that river below! Do you see how our king bears a keen wit?"

Midnight's face relaxed back into his customary sneer. "A keen wit, indeed."

"Glad to be of service," said Alexander. He shined his foreclaws on his waistcoat. "Shall we make her talk?"

Midnight sneered, "How quickly you've thrown off the bonds of romantic attraction, my little mouse."

The bottom dropped from Delphine's stomach. She stood still, utterly frozen. The world disappeared, and Alexander's voice was all she could hear.

"Romance? 'Twas but a game, a way to trick her into trusting me. She means nothing to me." The smile on Alexander's face widened. "I am entirely at your service."

CHAPTER 20

Delphine stumbled backward as if she had been hit. All those quiet conversations she and Alexander had had by the campfires, all that playful banter on the road . . . it had meant nothing?

Her mouth bone-dry, she remembered how insistent he had been that first night at the castle, following her and assigning himself as her protector. Was this why he had remained obstinately by her side through all the hardships? She thought of how curious he always was about the needle, and her magic. Had he been lying to her all along? Just trying to gain information for the rats?

Midnight laughed. "I think you've gotten to her, little mouse lord."

Alexander stepped forward, rubbing his paws together. "Even more enjoyable than when I defeated Fire-Eye."

Fire-Eye. Why did that name sound so familiar?

Suddenly she remembered Alexander's tall tale about the snake with red diamond eyes, and how he had pretended to be its friend in order to lure it to its death. Could it be . . . ?

Alexander crossed the roof toward Delphine, still addressing Midnight. "Give her the needle so she can show you how it works." He turned to her. "If she tries anything . . ." He pressed the tip of his sword against her throat and smiled wickedly. "I'll kill her."

Delphine gulped, but as she looked deep into his eyes, she could see warmth in them. The left one twitched in a half wink, and her heart leapt. She felt a flash of guilt for doubting him. She had been right about the Fire-Eye reference—it was a message. Alexander was playing a game.

And she was going to play along.

Midnight nodded at the guards behind Delphine, and they closed in, forcing her toward him. Midnight leaned down until his snout was nearly pressing against hers. From within a fold of his cloak, his paw emerged with the needle. It shimmered in the light of the moon.

"You think I'd merely hand it over?" He spoke slowly, as if he had all the time in the world, but now Delphine could hear the tension in his voice.

She forced herself to stare straight into his black eyes. They were dull as dry riverstones. "You will if you want to know its secrets." She let her paw slide slowly forward until she felt the cold metal beneath her grasp.

Trying to keep a frightened expression on her face, she carefully lifted the needle. The point of Alexander's sword remained pressed against her neck.

"Don't kill me, Alexander," she said, hoping she sounded desperate.

She gazed up at the moon, bright and constant, and in an instant the magic bubbled up inside her. It swirled through her veins and ran down through her paws. Keeping the needle pointed away from Midnight so that he would not suspect what she was really doing, she squeezed her eyes shut, praying Alexander was watching her face and understood to do the same.

She focused hard, and the needle blazed bright white for a moment, lighting up the scene in stark, blinding relief. She reopened her eyes to see Midnight staggering back, paws up against his eyes, and the guards all weaving in pain. Alexander was already leaping forward, aiming himself at Midnight's face, his claws outstretched. Delphine swung the needle up toward Midnight, readying a blast of lightning.

But Midnight was stronger and faster than both of them. He screamed, slamming Alexander to the ground and kicking Delphine away from the needle. The guards rushed forward, and Midnight waved them off. The scars on his face throbbed in silver lines. "How dare you!" He snatched up the needle before Delphine could reach it. Bits of froth sprayed from his mouth. Turning, he lunged for Alexander where he lay and grabbed him by the tail. Alexander twisted madly. Midnight turned to the edge of the roof, dangling Alexander over the void.

Delphine's knees went weak. "Don't hurt him!"

"You'll have to do better than that!" Midnight growled, the needle still clenched in his paw. He pointed it at Alexander. "You'll tell me how this works, or I'll use it the old-fashioned way . . . to fill him full of holes."

"No! You—you don't understand." She stumbled over her words, desperate to get them out. "I *can't* show you how to use the needles. Only the Threaded can use them."

"Absurd!" But his eyes flickered with momentary uncertainty. "*You* can use it, and you're not a Threaded. They've been dead for a hundred years. I know. I killed them all myself, right here in this very fortress. Your lies won't save you, little mouse . . . or your friend."

"You didn't kill them all," Delphine spat at him. "One

survived long enough to ensure the Threaded would live on. Threaded blood runs in my veins."

Was it her imagination, or did a pall cross over Midnight's face as she spoke? One eye twitched as if he were remembering some long-forgotten sorrow, but then the moment was gone.

"More lies," he roared. "More lies!!!" He stabbed with the needle at Alexander, straight toward his heart.

Three things came in quick succession:

Alexander sank his teeth deep into Midnight's paw.

Midnight howled in agony, dropping both Alexander and the needle.

And Delphine leapt forward without thinking, reaching for Alexander as they both fell from the edge of the tower.

Chapter 21

Delphine's paws reached Alexander and the needle in the same moment. The rocks were a dark blur below, flying up to meet them. Wind screamed in her ears. There was something flickering in her vision: bright white points and lines of light.

The web of magic around the fortress! She twisted in the air, aimed the needle, and fired a bolt toward the web with as much power as she could muster.

Silvery-blue sparks exploded at the impact. The web caved inward like a silk petticoat floating to the ground. As it billowed down, she and Alexander clawed at it, managing to hang on. The magical web swirled, wrapping itself around them, slowing their fall.

They landed with a thud on the rocky expanse that stretched between the fortress and the edge of the river. Mist from the waterfall filled the air.

Flat on his back, Alexander managed to speak first. "Thank you." His squeaky voice was hoarse, but in that moment, it was the most beautiful thing Delphine had ever heard. "You seem to be getting into the habit of saving my life."

"Only because you keep putting yourself at risk to help me." It was like a dam had been opened and Delphine was finally able to say what had been eating away at her for months. "I can't lose you."

He squeezed her paw weakly. "Delfie? I want you to know—"

At that moment, an arrow fell from the sky and lodged itself between two rocks, a mere whisker's-length away from her nose. Atop the tower, the rat guards were firing downward at the two mice. More arrows came whizzing toward them.

Delphine swung her needle upward in an arc, rage surging through her veins. A shimmering blue bubble appeared around Alexander and her. The arrows bounced off it, metal tips sizzling as they did.

"We have to get to safety!" The arrows were falling faster

and faster around them. Delphine struggled to keep her concentration and hold the bubble intact, but she knew she couldn't keep it up forever. A sudden movement at the base of the fortress caught her eye. More rat guards were swarming out of the fortress and heading straight toward them. She redoubled her grip on the needle, her paw trembling.

The arrows slowed, as if the archers had been interrupted. Delphine glanced back up at the top of the tower and couldn't believe her eyes. Bats were circling, diving low enough to harry the rats and in some cases even snatching their bows.

Delphine's paw fell, and the bubble collapsed and disappeared. They had to decide in which direction to run. To their left lay the river. Behind them and to their right lay the cliff. A tiny gust of wind blew across her shoulders like the touch of a gentle paw, but there was nobody else there. She and Alexander would have to figure this out alone.

A dark shape careened out of the forest on the other side of the river—Cornichonne, yowling at the top of her lungs as she ran straight for the water. She emerged from the river and clashed headlong with the rat army. Squeals rose into the air. The cat raised her head toward the bats, and Delphine realized she was echolocating again. She had summoned them to help.

From far above them, a furious roar split the air around them. Midnight was standing on the edge of the tower, staring down at them. The bats swarmed him.

Midnight leapt off the edge of the tower, into the air. He fell like a stone, his cloak streaming behind his body.

"What is he doing?" Delphine squeaked in disbelief. Without magic, a fall from that height would kill anyone, even a rat.

Midnight smashed onto the rocks, paws first. They could hear the awful crunch of bones breaking. He crumpled and fell to one side. His tail was bent at a painful angle. Delphine suddenly heard Elodie's voice again, describing the night that Rien had come to her chambers, beaten to within an inch of his life. How he had lain on her floor, gasping, fighting death. Despite herself, Delphine took a step forward toward Midnight's body, and another. What if Rien was still in there, after all? Alexander reached for her, but she gently pushed his paw away. She had to see this through.

Midnight began to move, stretching his paws outward. There came an even more terrible sound than before. His bones were knitting themselves back together, creaking and grinding as they did. She watched in horror as his legs straightened until he was standing upright again, laughing. His tail, no longer broken, swept menacingly from side to side.

He towered over Delphine. "You see, little mouse? You can't hurt me. Nothing can."

Terror ran through her body like ice in her veins. How could a creature this powerful be beaten? This was her moment to fight, but she still didn't feel ready. Behind Midnight, she could see Cornichonne surrounded by rats, battling valiantly. There were too many for one cat to defeat them all. And Alexander—kind, brave Alexander—she hadn't been able to save him, either.

The moon had dropped to rest on the horizon. The remains of the magic net lay scattered on the stones around them, slowly fizzling out of existence. She squared her paws beneath her and stiffened her tail. Picturing the faces of all who had died at the paws of this monster, she threw her heart into the black pit of vengeance inside her. It roiled up in a wave of furious loathing flooding her body. Jagged blue lightning exploded from the needle and crashed against Midnight's chest. He laughed, but Delphine tightened her grip and let herself fall deeper into her rage.

The lightning crackled into blue flames all around Midnight, licking at him. His cloak caught fire, but his fur remained untouched. It was as if his body was *absorbing* the flames. She clutched the needle, throwing bolt after bolt of cold blue energy straight into him. He reeled but remained upright. The network of scars that held him together began to glow blue.

"No!" Delphine was pouring all she had into the needle. How could it still not be enough?

Midnight's laughter deepened. He spread his arms, and the charred remains of the cloak fell from his shoulders, fluttering uselessly onto the stones. Delphine realized with sudden horror that he was growing taller, twisting as the magic coursed through his body.

"Delphine, stop!" Alexander's voice came to her faintly, as if through cotton wool. She shook her head to clear it. "Delphine! You're giving him more power! He's feeding off the magic!"

Midnight was already as large as Cornichonne and still growing. The power was no longer being controlled by Delphine or the needle; it was as if Midnight himself were drawing it out of her. She fought to let go of the spell but could find no way to separate herself from it. She had fallen so deeply into her hatred that it filled her body. It had become all of her, and now it was out of her control.

Alexander sprang at her and wrenched the needle from her paws. In an instant, the spell was broken. The blue flames died but Midnight continued to stretch toward the stars. It was too late. Nothing could stop him now.

Delphine felt the wrath drain out of her until she was empty. She had failed. She let her eyes fall closed in despair.

Alexander shook her arm. "Delfie?"

She pried open her eyes, feeling as if the effort was using up the last bit of energy she had. Alexander was holding the needle like a sword.

"I'll hold him off. If you reach Cornichonne, she can carry you to safety." He tried to give her a jaunty grin, but his eyes were wet. "Go!"

"And leave you here?!"

"You're everything to me, Delfie." Alexander turned to face Midnight, his jaw clenched. The rat had finally stopped growing, the last of the blue glow slowly subsiding into his scars. He lashed his tail from side to side, whipping up a cloud of ice.

Midnight sneered at him. "So you want me to kill you first, little noble?"

"You don't have the courage!" Alexander's ears were flat against his head, a look of determination on his face that Delphine had never seen before.

The thought of Alexander sacrificing himself to save her life terrified Delphine, more than the fear of Midnight, more than the fear of dying herself.

A realization slammed into her so hard she couldn't believe she hadn't seen it all along.

Love is stronger than fear. Love is stronger than hate.

Images swam before her: Maturin facing the snake to protect his family; Cornichonne staying by her through thick and thin; Bearnois protecting Ysabeau; Alexander leaving his noblemouse's life behind to join her journey.

Midnight crouched, preparing to charge. He snarled and his breath rolled in a foul wave over the rocks.

She stepped up next to Alexander and wrapped her paw around the needle alongside his.

"We'll do this together," she whispered. "I have a plan."

Love is stronger than fear. Love is stronger than hate. She could hear her birth mother's voice, over and over. *Love is stronger. Love.* Delphine's eyes glowed softly with cool silver light, the same silvery glow as her whiskers. That was what her mother had been trying to tell her all along. That was the way to defeat Midnight: not with more hatred. Not with vengeance. With love.

Midnight was upon them. Delphine looked at him with new eyes. All those scars . . . the marks where the magic had brought him back from the dead, so long ago . . . they had sealed themselves up with hatred and bitterness, hardening into a shell around him, causing him to calcify into this monstrous creature.

The magic becomes whatever it feeds upon. When the magic had fed upon her love for the world around her, it was shimmering and beautiful. When she fed the magic with her hatred of the rats, it turned dark and vitriolic. And when Elodie had poured all that magic into Rien, despite her love for him, she had poured in her own fears as well. Her fear of loss, of loneliness. Then the magic fed on the despair that had already taken root within him. It held him on the edge of the void, just short of death, but no longer truly part of life. No wonder he had been unable to leave this fortress.

If she could break open that shell around him . . . unravel those scars and release him from that prison . . .

She remembered her maman, Meline, back on the ledge of Cinderella's bedroom on that late summer afternoon: *Find the knot.*

Delphine looked at Midnight and could suddenly see that the scar across his heart was inky and twisted. There was the dark thread, right in front of her. She glanced down at the needle in her paw, tracing the symbols engraved there. *The Twelfth Knows the Heart.* She was the Twelfth now, and it was time to embrace her power.

She felt Alexander's paw in hers, warm and sure. She let her love for him bubble inside her, pushing away her terror of Midnight, her guilt, her fear of failing. The shimmering magic welled up like a spring gushing out of a rock, pouring into the needle in a silvery swirl that leapt forward, straight for that scar across Midnight's heart.

The arc of light hit him and he stumbled backward. She could see the sparkling silver flowing into the scar, driving out the darkness. She kept focusing, unraveling the magic stitches that had calcified with evil. Slowly the dark thread that held his heart together faded back to silver. He began to shrink down to his normal size, the cold blue fading from the rest of his scars until they all glowed with the gentle silver of the needle's magic.

Alexander gazed at her. "What are you doing?" he breathed.

"I'm *un*doing," Delphine said, still gazing at Midnight. He was quiet now.

She let go of the needle, leaving it in Alexander's grip. The spell faded. "Delfie!" he squeaked, but she stepped forward.

The rat's dark eyes watched her, unreadable. The now-silver thread was beginning to unravel itself from his body, stitches coming undone one by one.

Delphine's voice was soft and clear. "Rien?"

He blinked. His lip uncurled, softened. "How did you . . . ?"

She could see wisps of mist vanishing from his body as the scars evaporated, but she kept her eyes fixed on his.

"Elodie was my mother. She only wanted you to be happy. She loved you."

The mist was growing thicker around him as more and more of the scars came undone. His eyes were suddenly sad. "I loved Elodie so much."

Delphine no longer felt afraid. She reached out one tiny mouse paw. "Rien. Come back. It's over."

The sadness in his eyes grew so deep, it made her heart ache. "Rien died a long time ago." His form grew hazy as mist swirled around him. In a silent flash, he was gone. Silver dust settled slowly onto the stones in a heap. All that was left was the misshapen crown he had worn for so many years, nestled in the dust.

Tears streamed down Delphine's cheeks.

Then Alexander's arms were around her. "You won! Delfie, you did it!" He looked at her oddly. "Delfie? What did he say to you?"

She buried her face in his shoulder and let herself cry for Elodie, for Rien, for all the loss and pain. As Midnight, he had done monstrous things. But he, too, had loved, once upon a time.

Finally, she raised her head and looked at Alexander again, tears clinging to her whiskers. He brushed them away, still holding her tight. "You saved the kingdom."

She looked up at the tower where the bats fluttered, and out to where Cornichonne stood, triumphant. "We *all* did."

the Coulommiers moon

Chapter 22

Rats spilled out of the fortress doors, bearing down on Delphine and Alexander. She redoubled her grip on her needle. "I think we should go. Now."

But as the rats grew closer, she could see they were no longer carrying weapons, and they were headed by Mezzo, the clear-eyed guard with the notched ear and the blaze on her face.

Mezzo knelt before Delphine. "You have done us a great

service," she said formally. "We would join your ranks. If you will have us."

Delphine must have looked taken aback, because Mezzo grinned. "Perhaps you wonder why we are not currently trying to kill you for destroying our leader?"

Delphine closed her mouth and nodded.

Mezzo's grin turned bitter. "He was a tyrant. He pressed many of us into his service. And the others, those who served him of their own free will, are no longer welcome here."

Delphine managed to collect herself. "Didn't they try to fight back?"

One of the other rats guffawed. "Mezzo had them all running scared. You'll never find a finer leader than she."

Delphine gestured for Mezzo to rise. "I want to believe you, but how can I know you're telling the truth?" The needle suddenly sparkled in her paws. She gazed down at it, then back up at Mezzo. She realized that somehow, like their beloved Bearnois, the needle could read Mezzo. This rat was good of heart.

"Mouse!" Another rat rose. "I will follow you as well."

Delphine turned to him, but before she could speak, her needle shivered. She raised it toward the rat and it spat out a hail of cold, hard sparks. He yelped in horror and fled.

Delphine gazed across the group. "If you would join me, please come forward. Prove your heart is true." One by one, the rats approached. Those few unscrupulous sneaks who tried to lie were identified by the needle, but most were good and decent. They clamored around.

Cornichonne approached, and Delphine noticed the rats draw away. "Cornichonne is my friend," she told them. "I promise she won't hurt you, as long as you behave yourselves."

The rats' eyes narrowed. "It's a cat," one of them accused.

"And you're a rat," replied Delphine. "Until now, I was convinced all rats were evil. Turns out some aren't. Most aren't. So why don't we all find the good in one another?"

$$* \quad * \quad *$$

Delphine reentered the fortress, heading for Midnight's former throne room. She lifted the eleven needles from the wall and slid them into a sack. Then she paused, puzzling over a stack of round river stones that stood carefully stacked on the corner of the mantelpiece. They were covered in the dust of a hundred years. She left them undisturbed and moved on to the skulls of her ancestors. She rested her paw on the forehead of each of the eleven skulls in turn.

"I will make your kingdom beautiful once more," she promised.

She rejoined the others outside—Alexander, Cornichonne, and those from Midnight's army who had chosen to join them.

As the group wound its way back down the mountainside, Delphine overheard Mezzo asking Cornichonne about her musical background. Soon the two of them were deep in conversation about composers and songs.

That evening around the campfire, as Delphine was snuggling up next to Cornichonne for the night, the cat said sleepily, "Mezzoforte's nice."

"Mezzoforte?"

But Cornichonne was already asleep, snoring wheezily.

The rat Mezzo was indeed a surprise. The next day, as the group traveled on, Delphine discovered that she was fair to all. She even paused her troops when they saw a fistfight break out between two farmers in a field nearby. In just a few minutes, she had brokered a resolution.

When they were back on the road, Delphine moved to walk alongside the rat. "Why did you do that?"

"If I can help maintain peace, I will."

"But—" Delphine wasn't sure how to phrase her next question delicately. "Obviously, you're good now, but before . . . weren't you bad? I mean, I saw with my own eyes what the rats did. How many innocent mice they killed."

Mezzo stopped in her tracks. "I never killed anyone innocent."

"Oh." Delphine tucked her nose down into the collar of her cloak. "But—"

The rat began to walk again, clearing her throat. "I'm not proud of the things I did," she said in a low voice. "But I would have done anything to save my sister."

"Your . . . sister?"

The winter sun reflected in Mezzo's eyes. "When I was young, I was the best fighter in my hometown. Midnight had a habit of sending his generals to raid rat communities for recruits. Some joined willingly. Others . . . did not." She took a deep breath. "I said no, and the general left. That night, my little sister was stolen from her bed."

Delphine reeled in horror, but Mezzo was still talking. "When the general returned the next morning and said I must join Midnight's service if I wanted my sister to be freed, I went with him. What else could I do? I was told my sister would be safely returned. And I knew that if I ever broke my word and left, Midnight would hunt her down and kill her."

A devil's bargain, indeed. Delphine drew closer to Mezzo as they walked. "Your sister, did you ever see her again?"

Silence.

Delphine's heart broke into a thousand pieces for the rat. She let herself reach out and gave Mezzo's scarred paw a squeeze with her own tiny mouse paw.

They walked like that for a long time.

✳   ✳   ✳

Very early one morning, they crested a familiar hill. There in the distance rose Château Desjardins. The travelers had arrived at long last. Delphine was so filled with joy to be home that she broke into a run, leaving everyone else behind.

As she neared the doorstep, the baker's cart pulled up with the Friday delivery of croissants. Delphine scampered into the back, scooped up the best croissant crumbs as she had done so many times, and then headed inside the château walls. She knocked softly on the door of her childhood home.

"Oui?" came her mother's voice. The door swung open.

Delphine stood, clothes bedraggled and torn, face smudged with travel dirt—and arms laden with fresh croissant crumbs.

Her voice caught in her throat. "It's Friday, Maman."

Chapter 23

Her mother cried out, dropping the butter crock she had been holding. Then they were in each other's arms, laughing and crying.

"Sweet pea!" Maman said when she could finally speak. "Are you all right? Where have you been?!"

"I wanted to send word," Delphine sniffed. "But I knew that could put you in danger and—"

Her mother's eyes widened at the mention of danger, but just then there was a thunder of paws. Gus and Jaq rushed through the open door. "She's back! She's back!" Gus bounced in delight.

Jaq flung himself at Delphine. "Where were you?"

Delphine smiled. "With some new friends. Would you like to meet them?"

All three followed her back downstairs. A terrible racket was coming from the first-floor drawing room. "What *is* that?" she asked as they passed.

Jaq grimaced. "Drizella practices her singing every morning now, and Bruno howls along. Lady Tremaine and Anastasia are hiding in their rooms."

Delphine laughed and covered her ears.

She led Maman, Jaq, and Gus outside and across the front to the others, who were setting up camp. Alexander had already curled his whiskers and changed into a clean doublet.

She gave him a quick squeeze. "I want to introduce you to someone very special: my mother."

"Madame Desjardins!" He swept into a deep bow, charming the cap right off Maman's ears. "I've heard so much about you."

"What a gentlemouse! Our dear Cinderella is going to love meeting you when she returns," Maman said, smiling.

Delphine blinked. "Where is she?"

Gus and Jaq started talking excitedly over each other. "Cinderelly's at the castle to marry the prince!" "She went to the ball in a pumpkin!" "She wore slippers made of glass!" "He came here and found her!"

Delphine could have been knocked over with a sparrow feather. "*Cinderella* is the mystery princess we've been hearing about?" She laughed. "How absolutely perfect!"

"There's a human ball tonight," Jaq continued. "Princess Petits-Oiseaux is having a ball, too, and we're all invited!"

"A royal ball!" Alexander's eyes brightened. "I hope I'm not too out of touch with the latest dances. Perhaps Lord Ponceroy will show me a few steps." He pulled Delphine's mother into an impromptu waltz around the camp.

As they danced, Delphine crept away, heading back to the château. She had one last thing to do.

Back in her childhood bedroom, she slipped the bag with the other eleven needles under her bed for safekeeping. She thought of Elodie's words: *There had always been twelve, no more, no less.* Could the bloodline of the Threaded somehow still be alive, undiscovered for the past hundred years, unbeknownst even to the descendants themselves? Were there eleven other mice out there, scattered across the kingdom, whose whiskers would turn silver at the needle's touch? Perhaps one day she would find out.

As she turned to leave, she noticed the hooks over her bed where her needle had hung for so many years.

It was waiting for me to unlock its secrets, she thought.

Delphine pictured Elodie, standing on the chateau doorstep a hundred years ago in the freezing night, weaving a spell around her baby without knowing where it would take her little one, knowing only that any other moment would be safer than that one.

"Thank you," Delphine whispered. "You sent me to the perfect time."

The castle was in an uproar with royal ball preparations when they arrived. Delphine persuaded the rats to wait in the courtyard until she had talked with Princess Petits-Oiseaux. But no sooner had she stepped paw into the entry hall than she was swept up into a hug by Ysabeau, ears twitching with happiness.

"Oh, Ysabeau, I've been so worried about you, ever since Montrenasse-sur-Terre!" cried Delphine.

"Stop that this instant!" Ysabeau insisted. "You were double-crossed! It is *I* who have been worried about you!"

Delphine shook her head. "And Bearnois . . ."

Ysabeau's whiskers drooped. "I miss him every day." Then her expression brightened. "But there's someone I'd like you to meet." She pointed upward to a baby bumblebee floating above her head, his tiny legs barely visible beneath his black-and-yellow fluff.

Delphine squeaked in delight, and the baby bumblebee wobbled his way down to land on Ysabeau's outstretched paw. "Poppinot was born just a few days ago," she cooed.

Delphine reached out one paw and petted Poppinot. He was

as soft as a dandelion. He gazed at her curiously with his huge black eyes.

"He likes you," said Ysabeau, smiling.

They were interrupted by a flustered Alexander, hopping from paw to paw. "Delphine, hurry!!!" He grabbed her sleeve, dragging her behind him.

"Alexander!" Delphine cried. "What's the problem?"

His handsome face was twisted in distress. "Cornichonne's made her way to the human princess's chambers!"

Her dear friend Cinderella! She laughed and pulled on Alexander's paw until he slowed to a walk. "Cinderella is a sweetheart. Cornichonne will be fine."

She found the cat in the royal dressing room, weaving back and forth through Cinderella's legs.

Cinderella was giggling. "Where did *you* come from?" she asked. "What a sweet face you have."

Delphine waved at Cornichonne, and the cat came running across the thick carpet.

"I love it here!" snuffled Cornichonne.

Delphine smiled. "Isn't Cinderella the kindest human in the whole kingdom?"

"So kind," the cat agreed. "And a lot nicer than the cat who lives at your château."

"Ohhh . . . you met Lucifer when we were there?"

Cornichonne looked as if she had tasted something rotten. "He's awful."

"Maybe there's some good in him," Delphine mused. "After all, I thought all cats were bad before I met you."

"Nope." Cornichonne shook her head. "I'm pretty sure he's a lost cause."

Delphine couldn't help but laugh.

Cornichonne looked back at Cinderella. "Maybe I'll stay here at the castle with her for a while longer. She said she would have the kitchens make a miniature chicken pot pie for me tonight." Drool was already dripping from Cornichonne's fang.

Delphine kissed Cornichonne's nose, avoiding the drool. "That sounds wonderful."

Then she turned and darted back through the wall to where Alexander was waiting. "Now we must find *our* princess."

CHAPTER 24

Delphine watched from the windows of Princess Petits-Oiseaux's chambers as Cinderella and Prince Charming stepped out of a white globe carriage. The humans surrounding the carriage cheered, and the princess's paw-maids squeaked in delight as sparrows sprinkled rice over the newlyweds.

Smoothing her silvery gown, which was glimmering in the twilight, Delphine took a deep breath and tried to quell her nerves. Princess Petits-Oiseaux had already left to shore up some last-minute details, and it was time for Delphine to get to the ball.

She found Alexander waiting in the formal drawing room below. "You look like a fairy tale, my lady," he said as Delphine came down the stairs.

"Why, thank you." Delphine could feel her ears turning a little pink.

They headed toward the ballroom doors, where all the guests were waiting to enter. Clutching her needle, she rehearsed Princess Petits-Oiseaux's secret plan in her head. The princess had assured Delphine that this would be the best way to introduce her subjects to the new order of things, but Delphine's heart was still in her mouth.

After this moment, everything would change.

"Alexander? Are my whiskers smoothed?"

He gave her a winning smile. "To perfection."

The doors opened and the crowd surged forward. Delphine gasped, her nervousness forgotten. The ballroom—oh, the ballroom. It was suspended inside the main chandelier of the human ballroom below. Delphine felt as if she were floating inside a cloud of diamonds.

The princess stood on a dais at the edge of the ballroom, crystals sparkling behind her. Delphine made her way through the sea of attendees to wait nearby, ready for her cue.

Princess Petits-Oiseaux raised her paws. "My loyal subjects," she began. "Let it be known—our kingdom is finally at peace. The war with the rats is over."

The cheers were so loud, the crystals of the chandelier shook.

"We have among us the one who has brought this peace." She beckoned to Delphine. "I present the savior of our kingdom, and my guest of honor, Delphine Desjardins of the Threaded."

Delphine stepped onto the dais alongside the princess, and a roar went up from the crowd. Then the princess continued.

"She will be my adviser on all matters regarding harmony between the rats and mice."

Delphine gazed out at the sea of faces painted with a mixture of shock and confusion. She remembered what Princess Petits-Oiseaux had said that afternoon when she had asked Delphine to accept the role. "I need someone with enough heart to mend the rift that has been torn. You are that mouse." Delphine ran her paws along the runes engraved on her needle. *The Twelfth knows the heart.* Setting her shoulders back, she raised her needle high in the air.

The princess went on. "This kingdom can heal from the wounds of the last century if we work together."

"What, work with the *rats?*" a voice called out. "They've all magically turned good now, is that it?" A nervous titter went up from the crowd.

"I'm glad you asked." Princess Petits-Oiseaux gestured.

Mezzo entered the ballroom, followed by five more rats. A wave of gasps swept the ballroom. The rats climbed the dais and arranged themselves in a semicircle behind the princess.

"As proof that peace is possible between mice and rats, I present to you the newest members of my royal guard." The princess turned to Mezzo. "And their commander." The rats gave a formal salute.

The audience fell silent, the tension in the room as tight as a thread ready to snap.

Mezzo stepped forward, and Delphine shot a look at the princess. This wasn't part of the plan. What was Mezzo doing? But the princess remained calm as glass.

The rat cleared her throat. "Delphine is a hero." She stood tall and fierce, daring anyone to disagree. "She is *my* hero. She did more for us rats in one day than anyone had done in a century. We wish only to live in peace with you."

The silence hung heavy. Then . . . "Hear, hear!" piped up a little voice from the back.

"For Mezzo!" came another, loud and clear.

More and more voices joined the chorus, until the hall was alive with cries of "For Mezzo!"

Finally, the princess spoke, smiling. "Thank you, loyal citizens of Peltinore. You do your kingdom proud."

From below, the human musicians struck up the first waltz. Delphine could see Cinderella and Prince Charming entering the human ballroom. The music floated upward into the ball-room in the chandelier, and the mouse musicians began to play as well, weaving their melody seamlessly through the human music.

"The first dance awaits!" cried Lord Ponceroy de Clairemonde Villeneuve, who didn't care whether the rats were enemies or friends as long as he was front and center for the opening number.

"Oh, shut up—" began another lord.

But Princess Petits-Oiscaux cut them both off with a flick of her paw. "My lords, my ladies, I think there is no better way to celebrate than with a gavotte. Shall we?" She descended from her dais, signaling for the dance to begin.

Mice crowded around Delphine, all eager to share their gratitude. She nodded and smiled graciously, over and over. A familiar face appeared, and Delphine's heart leapt. It was Philomène, the old noblemouse she had met at Château Trois Arbres.

Philomène took Delphine's paws in hers. "Thank you. I can finally tell my family it's safe to come back to the mainland." She smiled knowingly. "They've been waiting for this news for a very long time."

Delphine blinked. "What—?" But Philomène had already turned and headed for the sweetmeat buffet.

The gavotte ended and the musicians began to play a slow,

romantic waltz. Couples took each other's paws, swaying gently to the music. Alexander approached with a bow and reached for Delphine's paw. "May I have this dance?"

And suddenly, everything else melted away. "With pleasure."

Alexander gave her paw a little tug. "Follow me." He led her down a staircase through the castle wall and onto a terrace outside the human ballroom. Cinderella and her prince were already there, waltzing in the moonlight. The stone balustrade of the terrace was just wide enough for Delphine and Alexander to dance alongside them.

"This feels like a dream," murmured Delphine. She was close enough to Alexander that she could smell his violet-scented whisker wax.

"I know," he replied. His voice was quiet. "I've wished for this moment for so long."

The sky was clear and the moon cast a silvery glow on the castle gardens. Delphine gazed into Alexander's eyes. "A perfect night with a perfect dance partner."

He gazed back at her, his eyes dark and luminous. "Agreed."

Their whiskers met in the kiss they each had dreamt about for so long. His arms wrapped around her, stronger than she expected, and she felt like she was floating.

"My lady," he said with a wink when they had finally pulled apart.

"Oh, Alexander!" She laughed, but she held him tight.

"So . . . you've saved the kingdom, rid the rats of their

tyrant ruler, agreed to be the princess's new adviser, but . . ." He paused.

"Yes, Alexander?"

He blushed right up to the tips of his ears. "With all you have going on . . . will you still have time for me?"

Delphine gazed at him, the moonlight reflecting in his dark eyes, and smiled slowly.

"Only if you promise to retire that old tale about the hawk-worms. You can tell a new one . . . the tale of how we saved the kingdom. Together."

Alexander gazed back, grinning. "I promise."

The clock in the tower tolled midnight, marking the start of a brand-new day.

epilogue

Valentine basked in the midday sun that streamed through the lattice windows, a grape in one paw and a short sword in the other. She nibbled idly as she watched boats floating across the cerulean sea. Why in the world had she remained in icy Peltinore for so long?

A shrew servant hurried past. Valentine poked him in the stomach with her sword. He yelped, dropping his tray. "Where are my prawns?" she demanded.

"C-coming, King Valentine." He scuttled away.

She laughed. When she had arrived in the shrew kingdom of Tarquor, she had told everyone her name was King Valentine as a joke, a mere jab at Midnight's pompous airs, but it had stuck. Now all the shrews treated her like royalty. No, this life wasn't bad at all.

Her fangs gleamed as she tore another thin strip of skin from the grape. Possibly in another month or two she would strike out in search of that cave that local legend held was full of treasure . . . or see if she could whip up a new army of her own here in Tarquor . . . but for now, she was enjoying these grapes far too much.

She noticed a familiar sailing ship in the harbor and sat up, her interest piqued. How long had it been docked? She chewed on one knuckle in thought. A mere coincidence, perhaps, but . . .

The door to the private lounge flew open and a lean, war-worn rat sauntered in. His tricorn hat was pulled down low over his eyes, but Valentine would have known that smug atti-tude anywhere. A slow smile spread across her face.

She finished her grape, then oozed over to the bar where the rat was drinking. He still hadn't noticed her. *Careless*, she thought. It was a wonder he had made it this far south without getting a shiv in his back.

"Hello, Robeaux."

His head whipped around. Shock flashed across his face. "*Valentine?*"

She shined her claws against the fur of his chest, then held them up to admire how they glinted in the sun. "Awfully far from home, aren't you? Whatever happened to spreading Midnight's edicts across the kingdom?" Her voice dropped. "Naughty rat. Have you been playing hooky?"

Robeaux gulped. "Midnight's dead."

Valentine raised one eyebrow. "Dead?"

The rat reached for his mug and took a long draft. "So they say. I wasn't going to wait around to find out. Figured I'd head south to seek my fortune."

"How very interesting." A plan was presenting itself, now that Robeaux was here in Tarquor. She studied the rat, recalling what she had heard of his prowess in battle. She was pleased to see that he stood tall and returned her gaze. So Midnight hadn't broken his spirit after all.

Valentine made her decision. With a rat like Robeaux by her side, she was suddenly itching to gather up that army. She gestured out at the turquoise sea, the white sands, and the city of shrews that sat on the harbor like an unguarded jewel.

"How would you like to be second-in-command in the kingdom of King Valentine?"

The End of Book Two

CODES

A B C D E F G H I J K L M

N O P Q R S T U V W X Y Z

ACKNOWLEDGMENTS

Delphine's journey onto the page and into your hands has been a long one, with so many friends, writing partners, teachers, and family members with me in person or in spirit along the way. I am surrounded by your support and love.

A tremendous thank-you to Brittany Rubiano, my editor extraordinaire, who can whip even the most overgrown manuscript into a perfectly shaped topiary of a book. You have the patience of a saint.

Many, many thanks to everyone at Disney-Hyperion for all your hard work. When I was a reader and not yet a writer, I imagined that publishing a book was a simple sort of undertaking. I had no idea how much effort and energy goes into even the smallest detail, and how many people play an integral role in that complicated process. Thank you so much to every single one of you.

To my friend Eric Geron: Where would Delphine be without you? Probably still just scampering through the forests of my mind. Thank you from the bottom of my heart for believing in Delphine from the very beginning.

Most of all, thank you to my parents for listening to this entire book over a stretch of multiple phone calls when I could not bring it to you in person. And thank you, Mom, for your years of service as a youth librarian in the public library system. I saw how many lives you touched with your love for all things books. I hope I can do the same.

ALYSSA MOON lives in Southern California with her cat Picklepop (the "real" Cornichonne). When she's not writing, she enjoys designing and sewing elaborate ballgowns for all those royal mouse balls she's certain she'll be invited to one day. *Delphine and the Dark Thread* is her second novel.

@alyssamoonbooks

Morceau

Flore's Camp

Dead City

Parfumoisson

Cinderella's
Castle

Château Desjardins

The
Deep
Sea

Bargeon-sur-Mer